COACH
A STORY OF SUCCESS REDEFINED

TIM WINDERS

Copyright © 2022 by **SGC Media**

All rights reserved. No part of this publication may be reproduced, distributed or transmitted in any form or by any means, without prior written permission.

Tim Winders/SGC Media
30 North Gould St, Suite R
Sheridan, WY 82801
www.TimWinders.com

Publisher's Note: This is a work of fiction. Names, characters, places, and incidents are a product of the author's imagination. Locales and public names are sometimes used for atmospheric purposes. Any resemblance to actual people, living or dead, or to businesses, companies, events, institutions, or locales is completely coincidental.

Coach: A Story of Success Redefined / Tim Winders. -- 1st ed.
Hardback Edition: ISBN 979-8-9858574-0-5
Paperback Edition: ISBN 979-8-9858574-1-2
eBook Edition: ISBN 979-8-9858574-2-9
Audiobook Edition: ISBN 979-8-9858574-3-6

For Og Mandino

In 1968, Og Mandino published The Greatest Salesman in the World. I read this classic for the first time in 1991. There are many events that impact our lives in a positive way, but I can honestly proclaim that reading his book changed my life.

I opened the small paperback for the first time late one evening and did not put it down until I completed the book a few hours later. I have reread it often since then. I have also grown to love many of his other books such as The Choice and The Christ Commission.

I was only able to meet him once during an event in Atlanta in 1992. He passed away in 1996. It is my desire that this book...this story will honor the legacy of Og Mandino in some small way and change someone else's life just as his stories impacted me.

1

The blue eyes slowly measured the path between the hand and the gun.

In the middle of the massive desk was a Smith & Wesson .44 magnum begging to be picked up. It would take the energy of a crane to move his hand. The seconds felt like hours as he stared at the gun while attempting to reach from the arm of his Italian leather chair to the marble top desk only inches away. That simple movement drained him as his hand flopped and rested on the desk's edge. It would take a few seconds to regain the strength needed to move again.

The eyes focused on the gun.

Twelve inches away.

Stretch.

Ten inches away.

Stretch a little more.

The hand was slowly inching towards the cannon that would end his life.

For someone that was always in control, his hand now had a mind of its on.

One more stretch, but still out of reach. The hand would now need the body's cooperation to connect with the gun.

Just six inches of space separated life from death.

His steady and methodical breathing were the only sounds to be heard in the cavernous office. That stillness gave no indication of the emotions swirling through his body. He had the ability to appear calm on the outside even when churning with stress and strain on the inside. Business associates and acquaintances said he had ice water in his veins and that he never showed emotion. Even those closest to him could never tell what was going on inside his head.

But like a volcano building up as it gets ready to blow, the constant pressure that had been forming for years was about to bust to the surface in a mighty explosion. If there really was ice water in his veins, it was boiling over at this moment.

His heart beat so hard it was straining to stay inside his chest. Sweat beaded up on his forehead, under his arms, and all over his body. The hot lava was making its way to the surface. The only thing spared from the glistening beads of sweat were the cold and clammy palms of his hands.

He leaned forward in his chair to get closer to the gun.

A big drop of sweat rolled down his forehead, over his right eye, and slowly down his face before falling off his chin and splatting on the journal page he had just finished writing.

His eyes locked on the Smith & Wesson.

A soft voice whispered, "Pick me up."

He slowly reached across the desk and rested his hand on the gun. The ice-cold metal suctioned to his cold, clammy hand bonding the two together.

"Pick me up" was whispered again. While the voice was telling him to pick up the gun, a force like magnets held the three pounds of metal to the desk. He was not a gun expert, but years ago he decided that he had to have the classic used by Clint Eastwood in the Dirty Harry movies.

"Do you feel lucky?" The haunting words uttered by Dirty Harry as he had squinted down that six and a half-inch barrel echoed in his mind. Cooper Travis did not feel lucky. He had every intention of using the powerful gun to blow his head off and release the hot lava inside in a massive eruption.

He lifted the gun and pressed the barrel end into the soft skin between his neck and his chin. The steel barrel felt even colder on his neck than in his hand.

Time stood still.

Everything moved in slow motion.

Should I be nervous?

His breathing slowed, and calm washed over him. The stillness in the air was eerie. Almost as if a presence had overtaken him as he was about to kill himself.

He took one last long deep breath, cocked the hammer, and pulled the trigger.

Click.

Nothing.

Cooper's eyes flew open, and he pulled the gun away from his neck to study its long sleek barrel. How? How could it not fire? He opened the cylinder and counted six bullets filling the slots. He spun the cylinder and snapped it back in place. He placed his thumb on the hammer and pushed it down as far as he could. When he made a decision to do something, nothing could stand in his way. Even if it was the last thing he would ever do.

He jammed the end of the stainless steel barrel under his jaw.

Click.

Again, nothing.

The pace of his breathing increased.

"This makes no sense," he whispered as he pulled the gun away from his neck to inspect it one more time.

The sound of a ringing phone startled him from the trance-like state that had enveloped him. A quick glance at the cell phone on his desk confirmed it was an unknown number.

"Not my Angel," he sighed.

He laid the gun on the open page of the leather-bound journal on his desk and spun his chair to gaze out the window of the office building. On any other day, the views from the Houston skyscraper would have been breathtaking. Today, Cooper sat staring at nothing out of his office window. His company occupied the entire thirty-eighth floor of the forty-story building. He still found it difficult to believe he had achieved his dreams and built a multi-million dollar company from the ground up. And now his world had disintegrated like paper in a fire.

Light streamed into the office from the floor to ceiling windows that made up two walls of the corner office. The darkness of all that had occurred recently kept pushing back on the light.

Two years ago, Cooper Travis would have been the last person in the world to attempt to commit suicide. Anyone looking at him from the outside would have thought he led a charmed life. He was the perfect example of a well-groomed, successful business executive. He could never make money as a male model, but he had that lean athletic build, giving him the appearance that he worked out more than he actually did. The small strands of gray in his dark, well-groomed hair made him look just a few years older than his thirty-nine years. He shaved every day and always wore a stiff, starched dress shirt and tie in a business environment. Most days, he wore a suit jacket even when the Houston humidity was at its worst. On his days off, he still shaved and wore slacks with a pressed golf shirt. Not that he took too many days off. Even when he worked weekends, that was his casual attire.

Today, he sat at his desk with his tie slightly loosened. The top button of his now soaking wet shirt was undone allowing some oxygen to flow into his body and brain. The blood had rushed back to his hands, warming them as the rest of his body cooled down. But the heat inside of him needed more air. He was suffocating from the stress and strain of life.

He contemplated whether he had ever known how to relax. He just moved from one goal to another and put out the proverbial fires when necessary. He assumed he could handle the business stress. Apparently he couldn't. At least not without his Angel by his side.

Cooper sighed as he stared blankly at the blue sky. His Angel was always so positive thinking and telling him everything would be okay. The slow-burning fuse that had caused the explosion inside his soul had started the day she left him.

It may have been the sticky, wet heat of Houston's August two weeks ago that had caused him to unload on her. Or it could have been the bad news that just kept piling up on him like hot coals. Either way, he had heard her say "it will be fine" one too many times, and he felt a rage inside that scared him. He prided himself on control, but he knew he was about to blow up.

"I don't think you understand the challenge of my situation," Cooper said with a sharpness that could cut through a solid wall. "It's NOT going to be JUST fine."

"I think I do. But even if I don't, I want to support you. This has been difficult for both of us. It hurts me to see you this way. I love you, baby, and I have faith that everything will somehow work out," Angel replied. The softness in her voice almost made him explode.

"I am not sure I can take this anymore," he said through clenched teeth. "I think I need some time to be alone."

"What do you mean?"

Cooper heard the slight rise in her tone. "Look, my Angel, I just don't think it helps to have you around while I am trying my best to save everything."

"What? How could you not want me around?" Angel's eyes pierced holes in his soul. "I'm your wife! Am I just supposed to leave so you can be alone? Do you want to separate? Or worse? Is that what you are saying, Cooper Travis?"

"I don't...I don't really know what I am saying." Cooper tried to keep emotion from his voice, but a tiny quiver was there. "I just need some...some space."

"I will give you your space, Cooper Travis." Her calmness vanished as her voice quickly hit maximum decibels. "I will give you more than your precious space. But you need to understand that I have stood by you in the great times, and I have stood by you when things were bad. I don't care if we have money or not. I grew up with nothing, and I can live that way again. I don't even care if you are in jail. I just want to see more of your heart. I want all of you."

"There you go again talking about seeing more of my heart. I really have no idea what you are talking about when you say that."

"Maybe you need to figure that out. Here is what I am going to do. I will give you twenty-four hours to rethink your request for me to leave. If you still think you need time to be alone, then I will move out and give you all the alone time you need. How does that sound?" Angel stared at Cooper with unflinching brown eyes.

Cooper knew he had lost control of the situation. He didn't really want Angel to leave, but now he didn't know what to do or say, so he said nothing.

"Ugh. I never know what to think, Cooper, when you have that blank look on your face. I know it helps when you negotiate business deals, but I'm not a business deal. It just makes me think you don't care. Is that what you want me to think? Because that's the way it makes me feel."

Cooper opened his mouth and closed it again. He didn't know how to change the expression on his face. He was frozen.

Angel shook her head, turned, and slammed the door as she walked out onto the back deck.

The next morning she had given him every opportunity to make up for the day before and to stop her from moving out. But he had no idea how to recover and apologize. He tried to talk but nothing came out.

Her leaving felt like a big punch in the gut, but he never let her see that emotion as she packed and left. His face remained stoic, and a smug thought crossed his mind. "She will be back. She needs me."

Cooper stared out his office window. He knew he lived a fantasy thinking that she needed him, because in reality, he needed her. His mental and emotional descent accelerated the minute she left. The more he tried to clear his mind and fix his life, the more the darkness closed in. Chasing after money had brought out the worst in him. If he had fooled himself about his need for Angel, what else was he allowing to deceive him? The last two weeks had been torture.

"I forced her to leave. Now there is nothing I can do," Cooper whispered. "Things are so complicated now. I wish they could be simple again."

He spun his chair around and picked the gun up from the journal. He flipped back to the inside cover page where Angel had written him a note:

The Tablet - February 14

Cooper,

I am your Angel, and I always will be.

You are facing difficult challenges now. Please know that I am proud of you and nothing can change that.

I know that you have never wanted to slow down long enough to write down your thoughts and memories on paper. However, I do wish that you will accept this journal as a gift that will allow you to share who you are in these pages.

I am honored to be your wife, and I pray that writing in this journal will help you become the man God created you to be.

Your Angel

He thought back to the night six months earlier when she had given him the gift.

She was already in bed reading when he walked in from another late night at the office. She had left the gift on his pillow.

"I'm sorry, but I do not have anything for you." Cooper picked up the small wrapped gift.

"It's okay." She smiled. "I know you have been under a great deal of stress and forgot that today is Valentine's Day."

He marveled at the lack of anger in her voice as he unwrapped the package and stared at the gift as if he had no idea what it was.

"It's a journal," Angel explained. "It will be a great way for you to spend time thinking and writing. Many people say writing in a journal is a secret to their success."

He stared at the leather-bound book and started shaking his head as his shoulders slumped. "I appreciate the thought, but I seriously doubt that writing a few words in a silly journal is going to make a dent in the mess I am dealing with." He tossed the gift on the bed and turned to walk toward the bathroom.

"Cooper Travis." Angel's voice was still soft but the firmness of her tone made him stop and turn around. "First of all, don't you mean that 'we' are facing? Not just you? I know that you are facing challenges that are tougher than anything you have ever faced in your life. I also know that I cannot begin to understand all the stress you are under. But I know we can make it through this. Together. I don't care if we have money, houses, or cars. I just want a husband."

She paused and her voice softened.

"Right now your body is around, but your heart is always somewhere else. I'm not asking for much. I just need to see a little bit of heart. You haven't given anyone a slice of your heart in a long time. If ever. Whatever happens to us in the future, you need to change. Your heart needs to soften so you can learn how to love. Cooper, I just thought that this journal could help you start that process."

Cooper watched silently as she reached to turn off her bedside lamp.

"I love you," she whispered. She briefly flashed that smile that made him weak in the knees, closed her eyes, and rolled over on her side facing away from him.

He stood for a moment before reaching down to pick up the journal again. The leather cover was etched with the words *The Tablet*. At the bottom of the cover was the subtitle *Be The Person God Created You To Be*. Cooper rolled his eyes, let out a deep sigh, and laid the journal on his nightstand before he turned toward the bathroom.

In the past six months, Cooper had only written one thing in the journal—a suicide note on the first page. He stared at the words in front of him.

The Tablet – August 24

I cannot express how hopeless I feel.

Everything I have lived for has come crashing down around me......

Cooper's eyes blurred and the characters on the page jumbled and spun as he attempted to focus on the words he wrote just thirty minutes earlier.

"I can't even write a decent suicide note," he whispered as he shook his head and stared at the page.

A short knock broke the silence, and his office door opened quickly. Cooper looked up from the journal to see his secretary walking in short, choppy, matter-of-fact steps toward his desk. Her steps slowed as she glanced toward the gun he was pointing at the ceiling.

"Susanna, I thought you left hours ago," Cooper said.

"I had some cleaning out and loose ends to tie up," she said. She glanced at the gun in his hand again. "Is everything okay?"

Cooper looked at the gun before responding slowly. "Oh...yes... everything is fine. I'm just doing some cleaning up myself. I found a few... a few interesting items in my desk."

Cooper breathed a tiny sigh of relief when Susanna curtly nodded and seemed to accept his reason for having a large gun in his hand. Owning or even carrying a handgun in Texas was not unique. In fact, seeing him with his tie loose may have been a bigger shock to her.

"I just wanted to pass a message along from Samuel. He left a message saying that there had been no updates on the sentencing. He doubts you will hear anything until early next month."

"I guess it would be safe to say that no news is good news," he said.

"I can't believe it has come to this. The seizing of assets, takeover, and shutdown of the company should have been enough. But to press forward with the criminal charges just seems too much." Susanna took a step forward as the summary of the last year and Cooper's nightmare punched him in the gut one more time. "Are you sure you are going to be okay?"

Susanna had been with the company since it started. Seven years seemed like such a long time ago. In some ways, she knew Cooper better than anyone else. Just the sheer amount of time they spent together allowed her to catch glimpses of what really went on inside the calm and neat facade that Cooper lived in.

Cooper nodded silently as she stood in front of his desk.

"Is Angel okay? She hasn't stopped by for your weekly coffee dates in a while?"

"Uh, yeah. She is traveling. She decided to go stay at a friend's house in Aspen. I think to get away from the heat." Cooper's words started to stumble as they came out of his mouth. "You know, the hot Houston summer heat. Not any other heat. She's not here. Not in Houston now."

"You don't seem like yourself." Susanna placed a hand on his desk, leaned forward, and tilted her head to the side making an obvious effort to read what was written in his journal. "I'm not used to you being this way. So unsure? Or maybe you are just tired and fatigued? Are you sure you are okay?"

Alarm bells went off in Cooper's head, and he slammed the journal cover shut. He glanced at the gun in his hand, then to Susanna, and then back down at his desk. He had heard the pleading in her voice for him to open up and share. He rarely shared what was going on in his head, and he knew now was not the time to start. "I am fine. Everything will work out somehow."

She gave him a slight smile and said softly, "Is there anything I can do to help?"

She reached across the desk and touched Cooper's hand that was still holding the gun. The contrast between the cold steel of the gun and the warmth of her hand sent a tingle up his arm to his shoulder. A thought crept into his mind as he contemplated her questions and how he could respond.

Ask her to have a drink from the liquor cabinet. Companionship would be nice. Maybe she will keep me from taking my life. I've screwed everything else up...why not add an affair to the list? Besides, if I end my misery later, who would know anyway?

He knew she was married, and technically he was still married. There had been some rumors around the office that they had more than just a work relationship, but he could not think of a time that she had acted in an inappropriate manner or even flirted with him.

And while she was attractive, he was always more appreciative of her professionalism and ability to read his mind when things got tough.

But everything was different now. Struggles can reveal strength, but they can also expose weakness. They can open up dark places within a person's soul that would never be uncovered without constant pressure. His dark places were opening up.

Stop. This is not who you are. Stay focused and get a grip on yourself.

A resolve welled up inside him, and he pushed thoughts of Susanna out of his mind.

He forced himself not to look at the gun still in his hand as he responded. "I have to think that some good news is coming my way soon." He paused, took a deep breath, mustered a fake smile, and waved his hand toward the door as if to say "get out of here."

"Be careful with that gun. You don't want to shoot yourself," she said as she turned to walk out. The sound of her heels hitting the marble floor bounced around the room.

As the door closed, he blew out a breath and leaned back in his chair. His eyes fixated on the gun again. Susanna's words bounced around the room as he shook his head back and forth. How did she...

He slowly turned the gun toward his neck. The third time's the charm, right?

A beep from his phone interrupted him. He instinctively reached for the phone with his free hand and pressed the voicemail play button. Maybe this was the good news he was hoping for. It would be great if he could hear from Angel one last time. Perhaps she had called from a different number.

"Hey Coop, this is TR. I know it's been awhile, and I hope I didn't catch you at a bad time. I just thought you would want to know... Coach died yesterday."

2

Cooper never really understood funerals or weddings or graduations. Why were they so important to so many people? They seemed like such a waste of time and emotions.

He had skipped his college graduation ceremonies because closing a sale seemed more important than spending an entire day waiting for a ten-second walk across the stage to shake a hand and get a piece of paper. And the one wedding he had attended had been his own.

The memory of his father's funeral was vague because Cooper had only been twelve years old. His lasting impression was everyone telling him "You will be fine, son." As he got older, he realized what people were really saying was "Your dad was a wealthy man, and you are his only child. Therefore, we assume you will never have to worry about money ever again." Those people just didn't know the restrictions placed on his inheritance. Baldwin Travis thought Cooper would be more successful if forced to perform for his inheritance. The family trust holding all the money had stipulations related to education, work, marriage, and even staying out of legal trouble.

Cooper had met all the requirements and cashed in at the age of thirty.

Baldwin's plan had worked. Until it didn't. Now, the inheritance was gone.

For only the second time in his life, Cooper was on his way to a funeral. This time for the man who had been a steady male figure during Cooper's teen years. Most of his players called him Coach. He hadn't really been a father figure or a father replacement for Cooper, but rather a strong man in his life that would kick his butt if he ever needed it. And most teenage boys need that from time to time.

The phone conversation with TR had been brief and a little awkward.

"Cooper, I know it has been a long time, but you really need to come back to Garland for the funeral," TR had said.

"Thanks for letting me know. And I am really sorry for your loss. But I have a stack of business issues piled up on my desk and getting up to the funeral would be a challenge," Cooper replied as he studied the gun on his desk.

"We have seen some of the news reports. I know things have been tough at work, and I am sure it has been hard for you. I think that's why you need to get away and come for a visit to reconnect. Hannah and I would love it if you would stay with us for a few days."

"Are you sure a funeral is a good time to reconnect?"

"You bet. It is the perfect time."

Cooper paused and took a deep breath. How much did TR know about his issues? And Angel? He had never even asked if Angel would be coming along.

"Okay, I'll be there." Cooper sighed. He sat at his desk after he hung up from the call. The gun on top of his journal was less impressive than it had been a few minutes ago. He pulled open the desk drawer and slid the gun off the desk. Before placing it in the lock box, he stopped. Maybe he should take it home with him. He picked up the box and set it along with the gun on the corner of his desk above his briefcase.

"I guess I'm going to Garland this week," he said to himself.

When a man is stripped of his possessions, his titles, his money, and even his wife, integrity may be the only thing that remains. He would at least be a man of his word and show up.

———

Cooper had made the drive from Houston to the funeral home in Garland in record time and had arrived an hour before the service began.

He took a deep breath and exhaled. The odor in the funeral home was a unique combination of clean, sterile, sweet, and musty. Cooper guessed that was what formaldehyde and other chemicals hanging in the air over thirty-year-old plush burgundy carpet smelled like. Combined with a bunch of funeral lilies, the smell made him want to gag.

But the odor did not seem to bother the crowd filing into the large chapel. They were filling every seat in every row and even lining the walls. The room was almost buzzing.

TR stepped away from the receiving line when he saw Cooper, "Hey man, how are you doing?"

Cooper couldn't help but chuckle at the fact that a man who just lost his father was asking him how he was doing. Still, he was hesitant to bring his troubles into TR's father's funeral.

"Well, as I'm sure you may know, my business situation is, uh, complicated." Cooper shrugged, trying to make his situation seem as light as he possibly could. But something about being in the presence of an old friend was loosening him up, and he couldn't help but blurt out, "And Angel left a few weeks ago."

Cooper stared down at the carpet and had a hard time looking back up again until he felt TR's hand on his shoulder.

"Cooper, I'm glad you came," he said with a slight crack in his voice.

"Thank you. I'm glad I decided to come. I...I changed my mind quite a bit over the past couple of days. I even called you to tell you I wasn't coming, but your voicemail was full."

"Let's talk more later."

Segregation still exists in the South. Actually, it exists everywhere. And Garland, Texas, is no different. As silly as it sounds, people that look a certain way tend to hang out with people that look like them. Hispanics, Caucasians, African Americans, Asians, and others all seem to go to school, church, socialize, and attend funerals of people that look just like them. Or at least that's what Cooper had always thought.

Coach's funeral blew that theory out of the water. The crowd was like a mini United Nations with every race and demographic represented.

Cooper did not consider himself a racist or bigot. He was not oblivious to the fact that he had grown up in a privileged world, and he had never been exposed to many things that were different. His private high school was Catholic and mostly white. There was nothing diverse about the attendees of his father's funeral. Old and white would be the best way to describe the small group of people that had attended. But when you are twelve, everyone is old, so his memory may have been inaccurate.

But Coach's funeral was not made up of the old, Catholic crowd. Or even the old, white crowd. Coach had left Saint Mark's Catholic School after TR and Cooper had graduated. He became an assistant coach at a large public high school in Garland. A few years later he was named the head football coach. He was the only option because no one else wanted the job of coaching a subpar team in a football crazy state.

But Coach was a winner, and he was able to influence and create success wherever he went. His teams did not win the championships like they did at Saint Mark's, but they won more games than they probably should have. And Cooper realized it was those students and their racially diverse families that were now filling the chapel to maximum capacity.

When an African-American lady sang a soulful rendition of "How Great Thou Art," it seemed as if half the people packed into the chapel were shouting and raising their hands. The other part of the crowd — the crowd Cooper fit in with — was doing everything in their power not to show any emotion or expression. Cooper had heard about holy-roller, pentecostal-type church services where people shouted and clapped and yelled "Amen" at any little thing the preacher said, but he had never realized those things would be appropriate at a funeral. He typically felt more comfortable with the sit-down-and-stay-quiet church crowd. That is if he ever were to actually attend a church.

The preacher said a few words, but Cooper's mind started wandering, and he really did not hear anything the preacher said. He did chuckle with the rest of the crowd when the preacher directed everyone's attention to the Folgers coffee can on the table in front of the podium.

Coach drank coffee all the time. In fact, he had a Styrofoam coffee cup in his hand all hours of the day, even when he was yelling at the top of his lungs to encourage young men to perform better.

Folgers was his preferred brand of coffee. According to the preacher, Coach had requested that his remains be cremated and placed in a Folgers can so that no one could stare at his dead body.

That can was now sitting at the front of the chapel.

After the preacher finished speaking, a family walked together to the podium. A young man in the family stepped to the microphone. Another man, who Cooper assumed was the young man's father, stepped up beside him.

The father began speaking in another language, and the family of six nodded in unison behind him as the young man listened attentively and then translated for the audience. "Our family was part of a large group of Vietnamese immigrants that came to this area several years ago. We arrived with nothing. No food, no clothing, and no work. We only had a few connections, and we were able to find a place to stay in a crowded apartment complex. We were in a two-bedroom unit with two other families. Twelve people total living in a very small space.

"Just a few weeks after we moved in, there was a knock on the door, and three men walked in with a pastor from a local Vietnamese church. Coach Walker immediately locked eyes with my father and became a guardian angel for our entire family. He started to visit us two to three times a week, and he would always apologize during football season when he could only visit on Sundays."

The father stepped back from the podium and motioned for his son to continue. The son transitioned from translator to storyteller.

"I was twelve years old when we came to this country, and I couldn't speak any English. The school I was placed in offered assistance, but it was still very difficult for me to learn English when so many around me were still speaking my native language. When Coach Walker started visiting us, he would sit with me for hours and hours. Sometimes, he would stay late into the night going over my school lessons and just talking with me so that I could learn to speak the language. Over time, I even learned to speak with a Texas drawl."

The young man cleared his throat and launched into his impression of Coach, "Sometimes a good kick in the butt is all a man needs to get going."

The crowd went from silent to roaring with laughter when he switched from American English with a slight accent to a deep Texas drawl. Cooper couldn't help but smile at the way this kid sounded just like Coach as he mimicked one of his favorite sayings.

As the laughter from the audience died down, the young man continued, "Since Coach Walker spent so much time working with me, he eventually realized my strengths in math. Thanks to Coach Walker, I am now a freshman at Georgia Tech on a full scholarship. I know without a doubt that I would have never achieved this level of success without the constant attention and guidance from Coach Walker."

The audience applauded as the Vietnamese family left the podium and a tall, attractive African-American woman took their place.

"Hello, my name is Jessica, and in high school, I was a basketball player at Lyndon B. Johnson High School while Coach Walker was an assistant coach. During my junior year, I became pregnant. When I tried to tell the guy who was my boyfriend, he beat me up pretty bad. The school suspended him for three days and made him sit out the first half of a football game. I dropped out and never attended that school again.

"Three weeks after my boyfriend was suspended, I had a knock on my door. And when I answered, there stood Coach Walker. I recognized him from school, but was unsure why he was there. Having an older white man standing at my door was a rare occurrence. But Coach politely asked if he could come in, and he sat with me and my grandmother for almost two hours. He attempted to apologize on behalf of the school, but he was also quick to point out that he was not representing them and did not support how the situation had been handled."

She paused and looked down at the podium, clearly fighting back tears.

"Everyone told me I should abort my baby, but something deep inside me wouldn't let me go through with it. Coach encouraged me to do what felt like the right thing in my heart, and he told me that no matter what I chose he would support me.

"We didn't see Coach often, but he did visit shortly after my son was born. There were complications with my labor, and my son ended up requiring a specialist that was not covered. Thankfully, my son is healthy today, but we were left with a pile of medical bills we had no way of paying. When Coach Walker visited, I let him know the struggles we were dealing with, and he was so nice and told me he believed everything would be okay.

"About six months later, I received a notice that all our medical bills had been paid by an anonymous donor and that I no longer owed anything. I never knew for certain, but I've always suspected that Coach either paid those bills or found someone who took care of them.

"Coach encouraged me to get my GED so I could get more education. He helped me apply and get accepted to a local community college. It was tough for me, but I went on to graduate from Baylor with a degree in Management and Business Administration. I was hired by a national bank right out of college and I now serve as a VP in Dallas. My son is fourteen and showing some skill in basketball. And Coach has always continued to call or visit us several times a year to see how we are doing. When I heard of his death, I begged to be able to pay my respects and share the impact he had on me and my son.

"I think back on that time of my life often, and we can never know how life would have turned out if we had made different choices, but I really believe that Coach Walker taking the time… " she paused and looked down at the podium as tears streamed down her face.

Everyone sat in silence while she stood still and sobbed. The seconds stretched to minutes. No one moved until the Vietnamese father stepped to the podium and handed her a handkerchief. The woman was at least six inches taller than the father, but when she turned to face him, they stared into each other's eyes as if they were both ten feet tall. She took the handkerchief from him, wiped her face, and then the two embraced as if they had known each other for years. After the father returned to his seat, she turned toward the crowd as tears continued to stream down her face. Her voice had a catch in it when she finally spoke again.

"I really believe that Coach taking the time to visit me may have saved my son's life." She barely finished those words before she dropped her head down again. After a deep breath and regaining her composure, she continued. "I hope it is okay to do this, but can I ask if anyone here today received some love like we did from Coach Walker?"

Hands started going up all over the packed funeral home. Cooper looked around in amazement. He always had respect for Coach, but he never thought that being yelled at and sometimes getting kicked in the butt would be considered love. He felt pressure to raise his hand so he would not be the only person in the chapel without a hand in the air.

A gnawing sensation began to grow in the pit of his stomach. His stomach had been churning from stress for the last two years, but this felt different. His bottom lip quivered slightly, and he wondered to himself if this was what emotion felt like.

Jessica thanked the audience and returned to her seat. The service concluded with a few more songs and a prayer. Before everyone was dismissed, the preacher gave walking directions to a gymnasium across the street. The celebration of Coach's life would continue during the reception.

Cooper knew funerals weren't typically considered fun events, but he had to admit that he had enjoyed the service. There had been something refreshing about the experience. The power of strangers sharing stories of how Coach had blessed them hung in the air like a sweet fragrance. In a world of selfishness and division, it was amazing to hear that at least one man was doing his part to make a difference. And he had obviously succeeded.

Still, that just didn't sound like the Coach Cooper remembered…

Cooper looked around the gymnasium and realized how fitting it was that Coach's life was being celebrated in an athletic venue. It wasn't the football field, but it was the next best thing in his mind. The man had dedicated his life to coaching and teaching athletes, and now many of those athletes were here.

Cooper leaned back in his chair and smiled. Since his business deals had been all over the news, he had wondered how many people at the funeral would recognize him. Nonetheless, he found himself relaxing as he interacted with old friends and acquaintances. Shame and embarrassment gave way to a smile and a chuckle. Even if those he was speaking with knew about the issues in his life, they were polite and didn't say anything. It was nice to breathe a little and forget about his troubles for a bit.

He pushed his chair back, stood, and walked over to a large display of photos from Coach's life. Then it happened. An angry yell ripped through the reception hall.

"You're the jerk that caused my parents to lose their house!"

Cooper turned around in time to briefly see a muscular man lunge toward him. Then pain radiated through his face as the man's fist slammed into his nose.

Cooper stood for a few seconds until his legs gave out beneath him. The faces in the circle around him swirled as he fell backward in slow motion. His next thought was that the hard gymnasium floor was going to hurt when his head hit it.

Then everything went black.

3

Cooper's eyes snapped open.

As he adjusted to the bright light, he saw purple and pink everywhere he looked. He vaguely remembered being surrounded by darkness just a few seconds before, and now he had been plunged into what appeared to be a pastel-colored bedroom wonderland.

As Cooper lifted his head from the pillow, he saw a larger than life Dora the Explorer on the bedspread holding hands with what looked like a purple monkey. He gingerly shook his head. Surely purple monkeys didn't exist except for in dreams.

He felt his face and confirmed that he did not dream about being punched in the nose.

He sank back into the brightly colored Dora pillow, and his mind drifted as he tried to discern how he had gotten to where he was. Not the Dora bedroom. That was most likely TR's daughter's room. But how did he end up in this helpless situation? He was even getting punched at funerals now. Could his situation get any worse?

Nothing seemed to be real anymore. But, at the same time, everything was too real. As if something or someone was punching him in the gut, not just his nose. And every time he would catch his breath, they would punch him again.

I still can't believe what happened yesterday. What an experience. I've never heard anyone spoken of like people talked about Coach. Did he really do all those nice things for people? Did I even know the real Coach?

He only remembered Coach riding them hard to achieve and excel as athletes. Or at least that is what it seemed like at the time. He had no idea what had transformed the man he thought he knew. Coach had faced some hardships, but Cooper's memory of the details was vague since he had left that life to chase money and success.

A tap on the door interrupted his thoughts. TR stuck his head in. "Did you and Dora have a good night?"

"Angel is not going to be pleased when she finds out I slept in the same room with a cute brown-eyed girl."

TR laughed nervously. "When was the last time you spoke to her?"

"Almost three weeks ago. It seems like yesterday, but also forever."

"Hopefully, it will be okay. A good breakfast can fix almost anything. Tear yourself away from Dora and come get something to eat."

Cooper did not know all the details of TR's life, but what he was looking at now from the kitchen doorway was as close to the perfect image of a family as he could imagine. TR was sitting at the head of the table, and his wife was sitting opposite him. Two girls, laughing hysterically, were in between their parents. Cooper struggled with believing that these same girls had been at their grandfather's funeral the day before. The comfort of the family breakfast table allowed their true personalities to show. When Grace, the oldest girl, spotted Cooper, she immediately stopped laughing and cut her eyes to the others at the table. The rest of the family attempted to stop laughing also.

"Pull up a chair and have some breakfast," TR motioned to an empty chair. His real name was John, but he had earned the nickname "Texas Ranger" or TR for short. Cheesy high school nicknames can be a lifelong plague for some people.

"Did I miss something funny?" Cooper asked as he sat down.

"Well, we weren't making fun of you," TR's wife Hannah answered while chuckling. "But we were having fun imagining the great Cooper Travis sleeping in a little girl's bedroom with his feet hanging off a small twin bed in a room totally decked out with Dora the Explorer decor."

"Why did you call him 'the great'? What did he do?" Grace looked at her mother with a quizzical look.

"He's been a friend of your dad's for a long time, and I've heard a lot of stories about him. He's practically a legend." Hannah looked at Cooper and winked.

"If they've been friends for so long, how come I've never met him?"

Cooper cleared his throat. "I think I can answer that one. I met your dad in middle school, and we became best friends immediately. We stuck together through high school, too. I practically lived at Coach's house all those years."

"Why aren't you best friends now?"

"Oh, well, I ... We went to different colleges and then life happened. I started a company and it took all my time. But here I am hanging out with your dad like old times." Cooper knew his explanation wasn't entirely true, but he wasn't about to explain to a nine-year-old the real reason. *Building my kingdom became more important to me than maintaining relationships. I never had time. Not even for my Angel.*

"Did you like my bed?" Becca asked as she flipped her head back and blonde hair went everywhere.

Thankful for the change of subject, Cooper turned to Becca and smiled. "So, you are the owner of the Dora the Explorer room?"

"Why yes, of course" Becca whistled as the "s" sounds moved through the spaces that would usually have teeth. "I love Dora, and I am going to travel all over the world just like her."

"I feel like traveling after sleeping in your room last night, too. Thanks for sharing your room with me. Where did you sleep?"

Grace piped up, "She slept in my room. I have a big bed, and Becca rolled around all night. She's a kicker."

"Grace," Hannah spoke in a firm voice as if to say *stop*.

"I apologize. I love my sister, and I love sleeping with her."

Cooper could tell that Grace knew she had crossed a line. Her matter-of-fact tone had not been sarcastic, but it did have tinges of "I will appease the adults, but I know I am smarter than all of them" attitude. From what he had observed, she thought she had certain privileges as the eldest child. She often corrected her sister, Becca, but always with a smile on her face and a motherly tone. She even let TR know that she may be the daughter, but she could pull rank and put him in his place occasionally. And TR seemed to be okay with that.

Becca was another story. She was six years old and missing every tooth that should be in the front of someone's mouth. While Grace's chestnut-colored hair was combed and pulled back in a perfect ponytail, Becca's mostly blonde hair was everywhere. She was constantly snapping her head backward and side to side to keep the tangled strands out of her eyes and off her face. Her chin rested on the edge of the table and both arms were fully extended on either side of her plate. Plus, she giggled all the time. She was quite the contrast to Grace who sat up straight and paid careful attention to not mess up her well-pressed dress.

"How does your face feel?" Hannah asked.

"Face?" Cooper quit observing the girls now that the conversation was focused back on him. "Oh yeah. From my friend's punch. It is sore, but I may have deserved it."

"Hannah wanted to take you to the emergency room, but I could tell nothing was broken," TR chuckled as he responded. "And even though you were a little groggy, you insisted we just bring you home."

"I guess my attacker's parents were the lucky owners of one of our companies now infamous finance deals," Cooper tried to make light of the altercation, but the table went silent. "I hope my incident didn't ruin the funeral."

"No worries." TR cleared his throat. "You want any coffee?"

Cooper loved coffee and proclaimed to many that he only drank the best. He had taken snobbery of coffee to a new level. He had his own "bean broker" that specialized in finding unique and expensive beans from all over the world. His roaster would prepare the beans and deliver them. He even had a coffee and espresso machine in his office. He really believed it made the best coffee in the world. Or at least he attempted to convince himself that it did. He often realized that he just wanted to show the machine off to clients and business associates. If he was alone, he usually made coffee in his French Press. He hoped that TR had at least some of the same love for the roasted bean. "What kind of coffee do you have?"

TR glanced toward the kitchen counter, and Cooper's eyes followed. A red Folgers coffee can was sitting there.

"I guess Folger's would be okay," Cooper hesitantly responded.

"Don't be silly. That's Coach," TR smiled at Cooper.

Cooper glanced over at Hannah hoping that TR was joking. She nodded in agreement.

"Dad loved his Folgers," TR tipped his head toward the can again, and Cooper's eyes could not look away from the red can filled with Coach. "He told us a few years ago that he had an old Folgers can in his kitchen cabinet stuffed with cash. He said when he died he wanted us to give the girls the money in the can and put his remains in there. He said we could just keep the ashes in the can or we could spread them out on the beach somewhere. He had a place on South Padre, so we may sneak him down there."

Cooper Travis was rarely speechless, but he had no idea how to respond. "Do you...do you have something other than Folgers coffee?"

"Sure, we have coffee coffee. What other kind is there?" TR walked to the Mr. Coffee machine on the kitchen counter and returned with a steaming cup of dark liquid.

Cooper took a tentative sip from his mug. *Ugh.* He poured in a heaping spoonful of sugar and a generous amount of creamer. He choked down a mouthful before adding another round of sugar and creamer. He didn't want to seem ungrateful for TR's hospitality and kindness since no one else in the world wanted him around, but this coffee was pushing the limits on his gratefulness.

As Cooper sipped his coffee and listened to the laughter and conversation at the table, he could not shake the thought that this family had attended the funeral of a father and grandfather yesterday. And his remains were sitting on the kitchen counter right next to the table! Something was wrong. They should be solemn, quiet, upset. Not laughing and happy...almost joyful.

"You want to go to church?" TR interrupted Cooper's thoughts.

"What?"

"You want to go to church with us? We leave in about ten minutes, and you are more than welcome to come," TR said as the two girls and Hannah stared at Cooper, nodding with encouraging smiles on their faces.

"Thanks, but if it is okay with you, I may just stay here and catch up on a few things. Maybe spend some time thinking about traveling like Dora," Cooper looked at Becca who was giving him a cute, toothless grin.

"Okay, girls, let's finish getting ready. Out the door in five minutes." Hannah gave the command and, in a few seconds, only TR and Cooper were left in the room.

The silence was nice for a few seconds, then it became uncomfortable.

"So, what really happened?" TR asked.

Cooper sighed and shrugged his shoulders. He looked down into the murky cup of coffee his host had given him. "Our company had developed a device that could increase storage of solar generated power. We didn't invent it. But we perfected it. The technology was cool and sexy, and it was destined to revolutionize the energy industry. The original technology was sound and worked well, but investors and venture capitalists had been pressing for improvements and new products. One of my biggest investors even forced a chief engineer on me. He kept pushing the envelope with aggressive specs to meet the investors' demands. But those products weren't tested well and were definitely unstable. Two house fires without injuries started the unraveling. The death of an elderly couple after a mini-explosion was the beginning of the end. We were once the darling of media and financial news. Then we made the national news for all the wrong reasons." Cooper unloaded from his brain in one breath without letting TR interrupt.

He wanted to keep going. The need to defend himself burned like fire inside him.

"Aggressive sales techniques had led to second mortgages being placed on homes of customers who bought the home version of our system. Of course, those homeowners may not have understood they were placing a lien on their property. Then some defaulted on payments, and when we turned the debts over to a company with little integrity, it caused a number of home foreclosures. Most would have never known about the mortgages if it were not for the challenges with the faulty engineered power storage device we had developed. Everything just started to unravel. Lawsuits, investigations, bankruptcy, criminal charges. It all started to pile up."

TR nodded with a slight smile on his face.

"It's not funny."

"Oh, I'm not laughing at your thorough recap. I was just letting you get it out of your system. I really meant what happened with Angel? When are you going to make peace?" TR stood up and walked to the kitchen doorway. He totally ignored Cooper's rant about his business issues.

"Oh...I think I really messed up," Cooper sighed. "She left me, but I told her I wanted to be alone first. I guess I pushed her away. She gave me opportunities to apologize. I just...just didn't know what to say. Maybe I don't know how to apologize."

"Give her a call. She's your wife. Go on and call her now," TR pleaded with Cooper. TR knew Angel, but not very well. Angel and Cooper had met about the time Cooper's life began a trajectory that would leave many of his childhood friends behind. Initially, the two couples had spent some time together, but when TR and Hannah started their family and Cooper's business took off, their friendship took a back burner.

"I doubt she wants to talk to me. She says she is okay with losing everything and even the possible legal issues. She says I must change, but I'm not even sure I understand what she's talking about," Cooper's voice trailed off as he finished his sentence.

"What's the worst that can happen? She hangs up on you? It won't be the first time the mighty Cooper Travis had a lady hang up on him." TR's joke to break the tension in the air fell flat.

"I'll think about it," Cooper replied as Hannah and the girls stepped into the kitchen.

"Will you be here when we get home?" Becca asked. Her wild hair was pulled away from her face and adorned with a bright pink bow on top.

"If it is okay with your parents," Cooper said as he looked from TR to Hannah.

"We would love to have you stay," Hannah replied. "Stay as long as you like. As long as you are okay with Dora the Explorer."

"Great," Becca let out a yell as she skipped her way across the kitchen to where Cooper was still sitting at the table. "Thunday afternoons are thuper fun," she whistled. "You can spend time in the backyard playing with us and exploring."

She wrapped her arms around him giving him a hug. Grace walked over to the other side of Cooper and patted his back. He suddenly realized he had no idea how to respond to the girls' affection. Cooper Travis could raise millions of dollars and negotiate multi-million-dollar contracts, but he had no idea how to interact with children. So, he sat still at the table with both hands gripping his coffee cup.

He looked at each girl and then stared at TR and Hannah with a look that probably resembled a deer in headlights. They just grinned at him.

That gnawing feeling in the pit of his stomach he had felt at the funeral resurfaced. Without even realizing what was happening and no ability to control it, his eyes filled with a few tears, and a single tear ran down his face.

And then they were gone.

He was alone. Again.

4

He reached for The Tablet and began to write. There was a time when Cooper would have had no challenge being alone with his thoughts. This was not one of those times. "I've got to clear my head before I go crazy," he thought.

The Tablet — August 29

I am still not sure what to think about Coach's funeral yesterday. It was amazing to hear people speak about someone in such a positive way. I doubt that many people would show up to my funeral. Much less talk about how I made a significant impact on their life.

It is so confusing because I was around Coach, TR, and their family, and I do not remember Coach being anything like the man they were talking about at the funeral.

He was a good coach. He could get more out of a group of teenage boys than just about anyone. That is why we won so many games against teams that were bigger, stronger, and faster. Coach Walker could get

> teams to dig down and just try harder. But yet, his athletic accomplishments were barely even mentioned yesterday.
>
> Something changed Coach, and I really want to know what it was. I am not sure if I can learn anything from it, but it may give me a clue as to what my next move may be.
>
> That may be the change that Angel is asking for?
>
> It is time for something to change...

Cooper put his pen down and stared at the picture of Angel on his phone. He had always loved her, but he never thought he needed her. Not like people talk about needing someone.

He needed her now.

Success and money can mask flaws in a relationship. Struggle and hardship can flush them out. That is what the last six months had been. A massive flushing of every challenge and flaw.

He looked down at his phone again. He had always thought she was beautiful, but her patience and understanding made her a rock star in his eyes.

Cooper pressed the "Call" button.

One ring.

Two rings.

Click. "We're sorry, but this number is no longer set up to receive incoming calls. Please try again later."

Cooper fell back on the bed and pulled the Dora the Explorer bedspread over his head.

TR and Hannah called their backyard "a retreat," but it was really just a small fenced-in yard where they relaxed and did nothing, something Cooper could not remember doing in a very long time. But the longer he sat on the porch with TR, the more relaxed he felt. He attempted to soak up the atmosphere and enjoy the moment as the late afternoon sun began to set.

He watched Grace sitting on a little chair in the yard with a doll in her hands. She was moving her lips as if she were talking, giving instructions to her "baby."

Becca raced by the porch with hair flying and arms moving up and down and all around. She had been using every square inch of the outdoor play area that included swings, a slide, a sandbox, and what looked like a version of a kids' fireman pole.

She ran up the porch steps to TR and gave him a big hug. Much to Cooper's surprise, she stepped over to him and gave him a hug totally covering him in sweaty hair. He usually hated anything that was messy, but the warmth of a genuine hug felt really good.

The sweaty hug put a smile on his face.

Then as quickly as she was giving hugs, she was back on the swings.

"It's hard for me to believe that you buried your father yesterday. And the girls' grandfather. Everyone is so … so upbeat. Some might say your family doesn't care?" Cooper cautiously brought up just one of the thoughts that had been nagging him throughout the day.

"I guess I can see that. Society seems to want us to grieve when we lose somebody. We just have a different perspective in our family. We spent a bunch of time with Dad over the last few years. He sat right there in your chair almost every Sunday afternoon. He thought he had only a short time left even though he looked healthy on the outside and never slowed down. He would tell the girls that there would be a time real soon that he would go visit heaven. He'd say that one Sunday afternoon he would be here in that chair, and then the next Sunday he would be gone. The girls would smile and nod as if they understood. He made sure they knew that they could be upset if they wanted to. But if they wanted to be excited and happy that was okay, too. Because he knew he would be fine, and he would see them again," TR's voice trailed off as his gaze focused above the activity in the backyard and off into the distance.

Cooper couldn't think of an appropriate response. He understood some of the church and religion stuff that TR seemed to be talking about. But he had been so focused on business and making money since college that it was almost like TR was speaking a foreign language. Seconds turned into minutes, and they sat in silence. Maybe he could change the subject.

"I remember Coach being one crusty, mean SOB when we were playing ball," Cooper said trying to sound upbeat. "Did he change or did we?"

TR chuckled. "Maybe a little bit of both. But I do know that Dad changed after Mom and Carla died."

"What happened?" Cooper blurted out as he searched his memories. He remembered hearing the news, but he hated to admit that he couldn't remember the details.

"Drunk driver. Dad should have been with them. They all planned to leave after school to make the drive down to South Padre for a spring break trip. He claimed he had to watch film from the season before to assess the underclassmen that would be returning. Just south of San Antonio a drunk driver almost went airborne coming from the opposite side of the interstate and hit Mom's car almost directly head on. We were told they both died instantly. Not that you need the details, but both of their necks snapped from the impact."

A wave of nausea hit Cooper, and he wished he had not asked the question. TR seemed to have no problem with the conversation, but Cooper started hoping that he could change the subject.

TR wasn't finished. "Dad was so engrossed in his film he never heard the phone ringing in the office next to the film room. Or he just ignored it. Either way, the State Patrol had to track down the assistant principal of the school to unlock the field house so that they could find Dad to give him the news. It was midnight when they finally got to him. He had told Mom he expected to leave about six o'clock that evening so he would only be a few hours behind them. After the shock, I think the guilt of neglecting his wife and daughter started to eat away at him."

"Neglecting them? That seems pretty strong. He was just doing his job, wasn't he?" Cooper snapped before he could stop the words from spilling out of his mouth.

They both sat in silence as Cooper's words dissipated into the thick Texas air. Cooper thought back to the funeral yesterday. The man he had heard described was not someone living a life of guilt and regret.

TR seemed to be reading his thoughts. "He went into a tailspin. The funeral was horrible. He sat and stared off into the distance the entire time. I would never say Dad and I had a great relationship, but he barely spoke to anyone including me for three months. They tried to get him to take some time off from work. But he insisted that he coach the team during spring football. He was so quiet and reserved his coaches and players were really concerned about him. You know how he was usually high energy and yelling most of the time. It may have been all the caffeine from his full cups of Folgers. I know you remember that..."

"Yes, I do. He chewed me out publicly in front of the team many times. I still shake from head to toe when I think about it." Cooper shuddered while remembering some of the blistering "coaching sessions" Coach had given him and the team.

"Well, imagine two weeks of practice and him not saying a word. He barely spoke to anyone. After school was out, I tried to check on him as often as I could, but he just would not open up about anything. In late June, I called him for three days in a row without an answer. I was dealing with my own issues then because of Mom dying, my job, and everything else. I drove to his house late one Saturday afternoon. I knocked on the door and got no answer. I pounded on the door and still nothing. I grabbed the spare key from under the flower pot and let myself in.

"The place was a mess. Dishes piled up in the sink. Pizza boxes everywhere. I was in shock when I walked in his bedroom and saw him sitting in the recliner in his boxer shorts and a dirty undershirt. He seemed to be in a coma staring at the bed. Empty beer cans were all over the floor. I never remember Dad drinking. He smelled and had not shaved in about a week."

"Wait," Cooper interrupted, "Did you say he had not shaved?"

Coach's football teams were famous for two things. They played hard and usually won games they shouldn't have won because they were physically and mentally in better shape than their more talented opponents. And Coach's teams were the most meticulously groomed young men that anyone had ever seen outside of military schools. And this was during a time when society was allowing almost anything to be worn. Shaving, wearing pressed clothes, and never having a shirt untucked was more important to Coach than how fast you could run or whether you could catch a football.

"Not shaved. Sitting in his boxers. He was a mess." TR shook his head as if trying to clear the memory. "I stayed with him for a few days because I really wasn't sure he was going to make it. It's tough to see someone who was a rock like my dad almost melt before your eyes."

"So, what happened?"

"One day he woke up. Just like that. He showered and shaved and told me he was going to his place on South Padre. I tried to talk him out of it, but he was as stubborn as ever. And he refused to let me go with him. He was gone for almost six weeks, and when he came back, he was totally changed." TR shrugged his shoulders.

"I don't understand. Totally changed?"

"I don't know." TR shrugged again. "He was still Coach, but it was almost as if he had gone through some life-changing epiphany. Like when people have some out-of-body, super-spiritual experience. He never shared many details other than mentioning a few times that he had met a man that was living in the lower level unit for the summer. He was sort of the opposite of a snowbird. No one goes to South Padre for the cool summers. But Dad said this guy caused him to rethink everything about his life."

Something jumped inside of Cooper. "That sounds like what I need."

"What?"

"A life-changing epiphany," Cooper paused after those words came out of his mouth. He needed to make a change. He had no idea what it was, but maybe he could find it the same way Coach did. For the first time in months, he knew what he had to do next. "Can I go?"

"Can you go where?" TR looked at Cooper as if he had just asked him to borrow a million dollars.

"Can I go down to the beach house? In South Padre?" Cooper asked before he realized he had raised his voice and was almost yelling.

"Sure. I guess so," TR responded with a puzzled look. "I'll need to check with the management company to see if there are openings."

5

Long stretches of nothing. That is what best describes most Texas highways.

According to the GPS, Cooper's route from Garland to South Padre would take him through the big cities of Waco, Austin, and San Antonio, but most of his ten-hour drive would be long and boring interstate. Shortly after saying goodbye to TR and Hannah, Cooper had turned off his phone, his radio, and even his GPS.

Now the only sounds he could hear were the low rumble of his BMW 5 Series engine and the tires on the road. Clack. Clack. Clack. The tires hitting the seams in the concrete was so steady and consistent it could have been used as a metronome.

Clack. Clack. Clack. Clack. Clack.

With no other sounds, Cooper was alone with his thoughts. He was one who usually entertained multiple thoughts at once, a skill that served him well in business settings but never with Angel. She could see right through him and would let him know when she knew he was present in body, but not in mind. He would apologize and work harder to focus on her while using all the people skills he could muster—eye contact, nodding, asking questions. But his mind would race back to the office, back to the last deal, back to the meeting he had that day. He couldn't fool her though. She knew but never nagged him over it. She just played along.

As he drove, his mind drifted from Angel to his business, legal issues, and even the last few days at Coach's funeral and TR's house. However, his thoughts kept going back to Angel just like a car swerves back between the lines after the tires hit the rumble strips.

Why did I spend so much time ignoring her? I'd give anything to have one of those minutes back right now. What a jerk I was.

Somewhere between Waco and Austin, his memory flooded with all their vacations and dates when he was wrapped up in business details instead of focusing on Angel. What a waste of time. The company and business were all but gone. He was going to jail. And Angel? Apparently, he had lost her, too.

―――

South of San Antonio, he stopped for gas at a truck stop. He tucked the box with his gun under the front passenger seat before stepping out of the car. When he went inside to pay for his gas, he grabbed a pack of powdered donuts and a cup of coffee. He allowed himself to smile as he took his first sip of the coffee and thought about the Folger's can with the remains of Coach. His smile turned to a grimace as the hot liquid went down his throat. It may have been the worst cup of coffee he had ever had. It was hard to imagine coffee worse than TR's blend, but this was worse.

As he stood at the counter waiting for the clerk to hand him his change, he calculated whether he had taken enough cash out of the ATM in Garland. He couldn't explain why he felt the need to pay cash for all his gas and food along the way since he typically used a credit card for everything, but he had followed his gut. *Maybe I'm running away. Wait. If I'm running, does that make me a fugitive?*

"Enjoy your journey south, sir."

Cooper dropped his wallet and change on the floor. *How does he know where I'm headed? If I'm a fugitive, will he call the police to report me?* He tried to steady his visibly shaking hand as he picked up his wallet and money from the floor and snatched his donuts from the counter. The clerk only stared at him.

He decided to drive north when he left the truck stop. He drove to the second exit before he turned around to point his car south again. His heart started racing as he passed the truck stop exit. *Did the clerk call the police? Did he memorize my tag number? Would the police set up a roadblock? If they search the car, they will find my gun. Should I try to bust through it or just stop?*

Ten miles later he realized he was acting like an idiot. The clerk was barely eighteen years old and was probably just trying to start a polite conversation. The south Texas sun and monotonous roads were playing tricks on Cooper, and he was letting it get the best of him.

To keep his mind occupied, he replayed all the events of the past year...with as much clarity and order as he could. But his thoughts continued to bounce all over the place.

His mind went back to the day before he found out his company was under investigation for fraud. He knew the company might end up in trouble for the issues related to the faulty units. He hated the thought that people had been injured and house fires had been blamed on his company. But the death of the couple in Oklahoma earlier that week was a punch to his gut that even he could barely handle. He prided himself on being able to allow any situation to roll off his back like water off of a duck, but knowing that a product that his company developed had caused someone's death was almost unbearable. He honestly hadn't known how to respond to that news. Of course, the couple's death put the company in the spotlight - the bad news spotlight. He had once been the darling of Wall Street and the media, but boy, can they turn on someone quickly.

The final straw happened a few months later when a court case was filed by multiple states questioning claims made by the business. The stocks dropped almost overnight, and the media was relentless. He remained calm in public, but unfortunately, he became a monster at home with Angel.

He regretted his attitude in many of their conversations, but he knew exactly which conversation pushed them both over the edge. That day, his stress level was beyond anything he could have imagined, and he had been attempting to speak in a normal tone with her. She was listening in her usual sweet, calm way. Then he made the statement that obviously set her off.

"I don't know why everyone has been making the death of an old couple such a big deal for months. They probably only had a few years left anyway. Why kill a company just because a few people died?"

A blank look came over Angel's face, and her eyes locked on his in a way that scared him. He knew immediately that he had crossed a line, and he regretted saying what he did.

"Cooper Travis, I love you with all my heart. And I know you are one of the brightest and most intelligent men in the world. Plus, you know I would stand by you if we had ten dollars or a hundred million in the bank. This situation we are facing is bringing out a side of you that I do not like. And I don't think you do either. I have wanted to start our family for the last few years, but the words that just came out of your mouth are not words I want to hear from the father of my children. You cannot be a true success until you soften your heart and learn to love."

Cooper had no response. He had always been in control, but now every part of his life was in a downward spiral. He held his breath and started feeling light-headed while he let her words bore into his soul.

Angel stood up, walked over to Cooper, and gave him a soft kiss on his forehead.

A few days after that conversation, he told her to leave. She walked out the following day, and he had not seen her since.

It had now been three weeks since that time. They had a few quick phone conversations, but Cooper knew that when Angel says she is going to do something, she does it, so she was going to honor his request and leave him to ponder her challenge—"soften your heart and learn to love."

Cooper sighed. He still did not know what that meant—*soften your heart?* He was a hard charger. He got things done. He really never made the time to slow down and ask people about their feelings or emotions. In fact, he prided himself on not showing emotions.

Love?

What does that word really mean? Society throws the word around like a bubble gum wrapper. People love their wife, their kids, their pets, and they love pizza. They love TV shows and video games more than they love their families. So how could anyone question his ability to love? And the bigger question was how was he going to "soften his heart and learn to love"?

As the sun slowly sank in the west and the monotonous low rumble of the engine soothed some of his worries, the only thing he knew without a doubt was that he had to get to Coach's beach house on South Padre Island as soon as possible. But he had no idea why.

6

What am I doing here?

When Cooper had arrived a few days before, the smell of mold inside the rental unit almost knocked him down. He called the property manager asking if the place had been empty for a long time. He was told someone had just left five days earlier and all he needed to do was crank up the AC and the smell would go away. After two days the smell disappeared, or maybe Cooper just became acclimated to it. The change in smell, however, did not give him any confidence that he had made the right decision to visit the area.

The condos could never be listed as a luxury beach property. First, the building was not on the beach. It was just near the beach. Second, it was built to withstand a possible hurricane. The exterior construction was almost entirely cinder blocks, capable of withstanding one-hundred-twenty mile per hour winds, but not aesthetically attractive. From the front, the building was shaped like a squatty letter "T." The horizontal top of the letter "T" consisted of two units that each had two bedrooms. The vertical part of the "T" was a one-bedroom unit along with some storage areas. Block columns supported the upstairs units and created covered space below to park cars on either side of the downstairs structure.

While the exterior of the building was solid, the floors and ceilings were paper thin. Cooper occupied the downstairs one-bedroom unit, and the units above him had families in them. He could hear every sound from above and at times it sounded like they were rolling bowling balls along the floor or jumping up and down on a trampoline.

―――

Since he had only packed a few dress shirts, dress pants, the suit he wore to the funeral, and a golf shirt, he visited the local souvenir shop to buy a beach wardrobe. The flip flops and board shorts were easy to pick out. T-shirts were a tougher decision.

"That's it," he said out loud when he looked up and saw a wall of shirts with "Hang Loose" written on the front in big bold print.

"Maybe this will help me relax," he whispered as he left the store with his new wardrobe. It was as if he expected the message on the front of a shirt to seep through and infect his body.

Food was never much of a consideration for Cooper, but he knew he had to eat something. He had visited some of the local restaurants that were a short walking distance from the rental unit, but he did not really enjoy sitting at a table for one. Instead, he stocked up on junk food, coffee, and diet sodas at the grocery store and decided he would just gorge himself while he was on his impromptu vacation.

He spent most days walking for hours on the nearby beach. He tried taking deep breaths of the salty air to clear his mind. However, the harder he tried, the more anxious he became. His long walks only reinforced in his mind how difficult it was for him to relax and do nothing. Waiting was not a skill that he was very good at either.

What made it even more challenging was that he really did not know what he was waiting for.

He tried to glean some wisdom about what to do next. The sentencing for his criminal case could be scheduled at any time. He could receive additional information about the company liquidation. Angel might decide to contact him. Or maybe he would connect with the mysterious person that was so impactful in transforming Coach's life. But Cooper had no control over any of those things. Lack of control can be torture for a control freak like him. Maybe he should have bought a shirt that said "Up Tight" instead of "Hang Loose."

His phone rang a few times, but it was never Angel. TR had called twice to check on him. Samuel texted once to let him know that there were no updates on the sentencing hearing. He even turned on the television, but nothing held his attention.

The longer he stayed on South Padre Island, the more uncomfortable and impatient he became. He tried to sleep in. But he couldn't really sleep. He just tossed and turned most nights staring at the ceiling. Maybe the heat kept him awake. Or maybe it was the thoughts that kept racing through his mind. Whatever the reason, as morning approached, he would cool down, calm his mind, and doze off. Then the party would start in the units above him and sleeping was impossible.

―――

Time can stand still when you have nothing to do. The hours became days, and the days turned into weeks.

On the first day he arrived, he had placed *The Tablet* on the small dinette table in the kitchen. He had intended to spend time with the journal and capture his thoughts in writing as Angel had requested. After two weeks, *The Tablet* still sat on the table unopened.

The box with his Smith & Wesson in it sat opposite the journal on the tiny table.

On a particularly humid day when the window air conditioner above the kitchen sink could barely keep up, Cooper decided to finally sit down at the table and open the journal. He glanced across the table at the lockbox and then wrote at the top of the first blank page:

The Tablet – September 13

He stared at the page. Not a single word came to mind to write. As he stalled, he flipped to the front of the book.

His eyes misted, and he felt the gnawing sensation in his gut as he read the words that Angel had written inside the front cover.

"Be the man God created me to be?" Cooper whispered, barely making a sound as the words formed on his lips. "How would I know what some god created me to be? I really need you, Angel. More than I can even imagine. Please talk to me."

Since he had no idea what to write on the blank page, he decided to call her. Maybe she would talk to him. Just maybe she had forgiven him, and they could just start over. He walked over to the sitting area and sat on the small sofa. The image of Angel on his phone smiling at him gave him that tingly feeling inside. Maybe it was a glimmer of hope. As he pressed the call button, he took a deep breath and held it.

"Hello, Cooper," Angel answered in a calm voice.

"Hello," Cooper replied as his voice cracked. It had been days since he had even spoken a word louder than a whisper. "I was really hoping you would answer. I'm down at TR's beach place in South Padre. Are you still in Aspen?"

"Yes, TR and Hannah called and told me where you were. I think they wanted me to fly down to meet you."

"Why don't you?" Cooper yelled. Maybe that was the reason he had felt like he needed to be here in South Padre. To get Angel to join him.

"I do miss you. But I do not think it would be wise for me to come visit. Have you enjoyed your time alone?"

Cooper wanted to yell and cry at the same time.

"I hate being alone. And I hate not having anything to do. I haven't learned anything. I feel like I am sinking in quicksand or drowning in the ocean. Which does make it seem funny that I ran here. Except nothing seems funny. I can't tell if I'm running from something or to something. I really have no idea what to do next."

"Then maybe you are getting closer to the person you need to be." Angel's voice was almost eerie it was so peaceful.

Cooper was rarely speechless, but he uttered a non-word: "Whuh."

"Thank you for calling. I really should get off the line now. You do not need me to interfere with your thoughts. I love you, and I know you will be okay. In fact, you will be better than okay." And just like that, she hung up before he could reply.

Cooper prided himself on keeping a lid on his emotions, but as he sat looking at his phone, anger and frustration welled up from deep inside him. He stood up and flung his phone as hard as he could against the wall. He had not really noticed the walls before, but when he heard the cracking sound of his phone, he quickly realized the interior wall was made of concrete blocks just like the outside. In a battle between a thousand-dollar smartphone and a block wall, the wall is going to win every time.

He walked back over to the kitchen table and sat down in front of *The Tablet*. He stared across the table at the box. The room became even more still than before and the heat and humidity suddenly increased. The feeling he felt back in his office began to creep back on him.

Open up the box and pick up the gun.

Cooper took a deep breath. Air flowed back to his brain.

His eyes snapped away from the box and down to *The Tablet* under his nose. He stared at the words on the cover.

"Be the person God created you to be," he whispered.

He flipped the page and read his suicide note from weeks earlier. Cooper became light-headed while reading the note.

He flipped back to the page where he had written *September 13* earlier. In big bold print, he wrote four words on the page and then stared at them for several minutes.

He was defeated. He was beaten. He was broken.

He had no idea what to do next.

Cooper Travis closed the journal, stood up, turned out the lights, and walked out the door without even locking it.

7

South Padre Island is only about four blocks wide in most places. Coach's condo was only a block and a half from the beach. Cooper could have just walked along the beach like he had been doing almost every day for the past two weeks. Instead he walked to Padre Boulevard and turned right to head north. He wasn't sure where he was going, but after he passed an amusement park with a go-kart track, he saw a sign pointing left that said "Beer By The Bay."

His mouth watered at the thought of a good whiskey or Scotch. He never drank much. Coffee was his vice. And diet sodas from time to time. But he needed a drink. Eleven o'clock in the morning. A beer would be good. Or two. Maybe more.

As he pulled out a stool from the bar, a couple nodded in his direction. He glanced around the outdoor patio with its faded pastel paint. The place was almost empty, sticky floors, and a mixture of saltwater, fish, and stale beer in the air. Classic beach bar.

Cooper smiled. The beachy vibes couldn't scare him away now. He was focused and wanted a late morning beer. Eleven o'clock used to mean Susanna would bring him his third cup of coffee from his high-dollar machine at the office. He snorted. *How the mighty have fallen.* He couldn't even get the young bartender to acknowledge him.

After what seemed like ten minutes, the bartender finally asked him if he wanted anything.

How many people come to sit in the Beer By The Bay in the morning that do not want anything?

"Do you have any locally brewed beers?" Cooper asked. He immediately realized that may not have been a good question based on the look on the bartender's face.

"Not really."

"What do you have on draft?"

"Bud, Bud Light, and PBR," replied the twenty-something-year-old bartender in the most monotone, I-don't-care voice Cooper had ever heard.

Can life get any worse? God must be punishing me. Cooper decided not to fight the punishment. "Give me a Pabst Blue Ribbon."

The bartender muttered something about PBR being really popular now with the young, cool crowd as he sloshed the beer in front of Cooper in a plastic cup.

"Do you have glasses or a mug?"

"Nope, just plastic," replied the bartender.

Cooper felt as if he was on a downward spiral that kept picking up steam. Will it ever end?

Cooper stared at the beer for a moment before turning it up and chugging almost half the cup. The beer was warm and almost made him gag. But he kept drinking. As he returned the cup to the bar, an eerie sensation came over him. And the sensation was not from the heinous liquid racing to his stomach. Someone was watching him.

Cooper slowly turned his head to the right and spotted a bearded man, seated at the far corner of the bar, staring directly at him. Not wanting to stare back, Cooper jerked his eyes back to the half empty cup in front of him. He turned up the cup and finished it in a few gulps. Oddly enough the second swig went down a little bit smoother than the first.

He pointed to the bartender and then his cup to let the bartender know he wanted another. *Because punishing one's self can be enjoyable at times.*

Cooper let his thoughts wander as he drank his second cup. *Why is the man staring at me? Am I being followed? Am I now a fugitive? Or, is this the mysterious man that changed Coach's life?*

He glanced back to his right.

No one was there.

The bar was empty.

Cooper scanned all around the restaurant, and he only saw the couple seated at a table on the porch by the bay.

"What happened to the guy at the end of the bar?" Cooper asked the bartender.

"What guy?"

"The bearded gentleman that was just sitting right there," Cooper pointed as he raised his voice just a little too much.

"I don't remember anybody there. You're the only dude that's been here at the bar this morning. You need to hang loose, brah," He chuckled as he glanced down at Cooper's shirt.

Cooper went silent.

I'm going crazy. Maybe even hallucinating. Could PBR have that much effect on the brain in five minutes?

Cooper drank one more beer from the plastic cup. He could almost feel the warm beer run through his body.

"How much?" he asked the bartender as he pointed to his plastic cup.

"Twenty-one dollars."

"Seven bucks for a warm Pabst Blue Ribbon in a plastic cup? "

"Welcome to beach prices," the bartender replied with a more monotone voice than he had previously used.

Cooper laid his credit card on the bar and headed to the restroom. When he returned, the bartender handed him his card.

"This card's no good, man. It was re-jec-ted."

When he said the word "rejected," he seemed to drag the word out a few seconds longer and also add more emotion than he had exhibited the entire time Cooper had been at the bar.

Frozen.

Cooper's attorney had warned him that the IRS may freeze his accounts. Now he knew that was confirmed. But worse, now they knew where he was. They track those sorts of things, and someone awaiting sentencing that is spending time twenty minutes from the Mexican border could be red flagged as a flight risk.

"I think I have some cash," Cooper muttered as he looked in his wallet only to see one twenty-dollar bill left from the cash he had pulled from the ATM in Garland.

"My apologies, but all I have is twenty."

"You have any other cards?" The laid-back demeanor had now vanished. The bartender had jumped to an almost militant "don't mess with my money" attitude.

Cooper knew all his other cards were locked and frozen. "Here's a twenty, take it or leave it."

Cooper's mind flashed back to a little over two years ago when he was negotiating with the United States government to provide power storage for every government property that utilized solar in North America. He even negotiated a first right of refusal for every military base in the world. That contract was for more than a billion dollars.

Now he was negotiating with a beach bum bartender over three warm beers.

Cooper tried to stand up straight and exhibit a small amount of dignity in his beach outfit. But he felt like crawling under the bar. Or running and jumping in the bay.

After a twenty-second stare down, the bartender said, "I'm pissed off, but give me the twenty dollars."

Cooper handed him the money and attempted to say "I appreciate it," but words did not come out of his mouth. It could be that he was shocked that he was being forced to give thanks for the transaction that had just occurred.

As he walked south on Padre Boulevard, he occasionally glanced over his shoulder to make sure he wasn't being followed. His feet seemed to have a mind of their own as he tried to walk at a steady pace. He knew he wasn't drunk or even buzzed after drinking the PBR, but his nerves sure were messing with him.

About a block from his rental unit, he stopped to wait for the traffic to clear so he could turn left to cross the road. The same uneasiness he experienced at the bar crept up his spine.

He was being watched again.

Cooper glanced to his right and spotted the same bearded man from the end of the bar. For reasons unknown, Cooper quickly turned and looked straight ahead.

What is going on? Am I crazy? Maybe the beer affected me more than I thought. Am I really being followed? Who is this guy?

He took a deep breath and forced himself to look back to his right. His heart sank.

No one there.

He walked the final block to the rental unit. By the time he reached the door, his heart was racing, and his breaths came shorter and faster by the second. He leaned against the door and twisted the knob. Nothing happened. He shoved harder. His body hit the immovable door. He tried turning the knob again.

Locked.

Cooper pulled the key from his pocket, twisted it in the keyhole, and swung the door open.

"I know I left this door unlocked," he whispered.

He took a couple of deep breaths attempting to calm his racing heart. His knees almost buckled, and he felt the sweat forming on his palms. Something was wrong.

He stood just inside the door. Frozen. Unable to move. He scanned the main room. Someone had been there since he had left. That's the only way the door could have been locked without a key—from the inside. He held his breath. *Were they still there?*

He took two steps and looked to his left. The bedroom light was off. He held his breath and flipped the light switch. He quickly scanned the room and noticed nothing out of order. He even looked under the bed and in the adjoining bathroom.

Nothing.

He slowly walked back to the main room.

Then he noticed it. The light was on above the kitchen table.

I know I turned that off earlier.

He stepped toward the table. Crunch. He jumped back only to see a piece of his phone where his foot had just been.

He glanced over his shoulder. He kept thinking someone else was in the room. But no one was there.

He refocused on the kitchen table. *The Tablet* was still lying where he left it. His pen was there too. The box with his gun was in the same spot he left it. Then he saw it. An envelope sticking out of the journal.

He sank into the closest chair. His hand shook as he reached for *The Tablet*. He took another long deep breath and opened it to the spot where the envelope marked a page.

September 13. He whispered the four words he had written on the page a few hours earlier.

Then his eyes shifted to the envelope.

   Mr. Cooper Travis

His name was handwritten. Or at least he thought it was. Cooper angled the envelope toward the light to see if it was machine printed. The slight feathering of the ink told him someone had very distinct and neat handwriting.

He turned the envelope over and broke the wax seal. *That's not something you see every day. A wax seal on an envelope. I didn't realize people still used them except for formal invitations.*

He pulled a folded piece of paper out of the envelope. He knew quality when he felt it, and this paper was some of the finest. He unfolded the paper and scanned a page full of what appeared to be details and instructions.

At the top of the page written in the same distinct handwriting as the envelope were the words:

Do you trust me?

8

One week later.

Was it possible for the brain to overheat and melt?

Fire burned through his body from the inside out. His eyes felt so hot and full of pressure he thought they might pop out of their sockets. The heat inside his head was intense. His entire body tingled and ached.

A fever. A fever like he had never known.

He drifted in and out of consciousness losing track of where he was, what day it was, and even what time it was.

Deep sleep. Cold sweats. Vivid dreams.

In one dream, Cooper is walking down a long corridor to a massive door. The door opens automatically revealing a courtroom full of people. A tall judge's bench stands on the opposite side of the room.

The crowd murmurs and whispers as Cooper slowly makes his way to the judge's bench. He is gliding, not walking, almost as if something were pulling him through the gallery. He is moving quickly, but it takes forever to reach the other side of the room.

When he stops in front of the bench, his head tilts backward to see all the way to the top where a judge sits with a gavel held high in his hand.

"Cooper Travis. You are guilty. Guilty. Guilty." The judge yells over and over again while banging the gavel. The crowd joins in chanting, "Guilty. Guilty. Guilty."

The room goes completely dark as the chanting fades off into the distance.

A loud alarm sounds. Red lights flash on and off, on and off.

Cooper steps into a small cell. Just a simple, metal cot with a thin mattress sits against the wall.

He hears a swoosh behind him and turns in time to see the bars of the jail cell door slam shut.

The clanking explosion of metal against metal forces him to backpedal a few steps.

He is locked up. In jail. A prisoner.

―――

Cooper felt a presence just above his head.

His eyes were closed, but he knew it was the bearded man staring at him.

Is this a dream? Or is it real?

A hand touched his hot, sweaty forehead. Muffled sounds came from just a few inches in front of his face. He strained to see, but his eyes would not open. They felt so heavy.

Every muscle in his body struggled to support opening his eyes. *If I could just get them open.*

His effort began to pay off as he felt his eyelids flutter and quiver. Seconds passed before the energy rushing to his eyelids finally forced them open.

As Cooper's eyes opened, his suspicions were confirmed. The face of the bearded man was less than twelve inches from his face. The man's hand rested on Cooper's forehead. His eyes were closed, and he was whispering something under his breath.

Cooper wanted to jump up and run, but his body refused to move. Something even heavier than gravity held his body down on the bed. The only thing working were his eyes. And they were staring at a stranger directly in front of them.

The bearded man's eyes stayed closed for just a few moments and then he opened them and peered right into Cooper's eyes. Deep into them. The man's eyes were a bottomless sea of deep blue. Then he gave Cooper a slight grin.

Any anxiety that Cooper had disappeared. At least for that brief moment. The heat that had been in his body began to melt away. Peace and calm washed over Cooper's body like soft waves.

"Get some rest, Mr. Travis. You will need it," said the man as he stood up and walked away.

Cooper had a brief thought that he should get up and follow him. But he let out a long deep breath and fell asleep before the breath even left his body.

Cooper could not remember when he had last slept through the night. He had spent years jacked up on adrenaline or caffeine and, more recently, staring at the ceiling allowing anxiety to rule his life.

Now, he was lying in a luxurious bed feeling more rested than he had felt in years. In fact, possibly ever. He was not sure how long he had been asleep, but he was confident it had been over twenty-four hours. The events of the last few days were a blur…almost surreal.

His stomach rumbled from hunger. *When did I last eat?*

He searched his mind for clues about where he was and how he got here.

For some reason, Cooper never even paused when he read the words written on the top of the paper at the kitchen table of the South Padre condo: *Do you trust me?*

Something inside urged him to do whatever the instructions said.

Cooper had spent his entire life living by rules, and in many ways doing what he thought the world, society, and other people thought he should do. Of course, there were times he made up his own rules, but that's another story. *Spontaneous* was not a word that anyone would use to describe Cooper Travis.

But yet, when he read the first line of instruction — *Leave everything behind; take nothing for your journey* — he went to the bedroom, undressed, took a quick shower, and put on his dress shoes, dress pants, and his Hang Loose T-shirt with a dress shirt over it. He emptied his pockets, and then packed the rest of his stuff in his bag and left it sitting on the bed. His phone was still in pieces on the floor, so he wasn't tempted to take it along. The only thing he planned to carry out the door was *The Tablet* and the paper with his instructions tucked inside. He glanced at the gun sitting on the table.

"It's time to leave everything behind," he said as he gazed at the gun box.

I'd have to be crazy to believe this. It's definitely farfetched. I may as well play along. It beats sitting around here waiting. Cooper read the instructions through again as he walked toward the door.

Do you trust me?

Leave everything behind; take nothing for your journey.

You have a divine appointment in Costa Rica.

There is nothing that you currently own that will be required for this journey other than faith.

Do not bring money or identification.

Do not bring extra clothing.

Do not bring food.

Leave your possessions and dress for travel.

Walk to the main road and turn left toward the south.

You will receive further instructions as you travel. These words will have meaning along your path:

- Mini Cooper

- Whataburger

- Carmen

- Bus

- Jesus

Enjoy your journey. We will meet soon.

After one final glance around the rental unit, he walked out, locked the door, and hid the key. He stopped at his car which had been sitting under the covered carport the entire time he had been on the island. He checked both doors to make sure they were locked. Leaving a BMW sitting in a vacation rental property driveway isn't typical, but neither is attempting to travel to Costa Rica without identification or a passport. Cooper shrugged. *What do I have to lose? I'm going to prison before long anyway. May as well see what adventure awaits.*

Cooper walked to the corner and turned left to head south. The instructions sounded like he would know what to do next. Cooper chuckled as he walked. *This may become the shortest adventure ever.*

His pace slowed as he played mental ping pong. *What am I doing? This isn't a good idea.*

He had almost convinced himself to turn around when a car slowed down and the passenger window opened.

"Do you need a lift to Brownsville?" the elderly lady asked as she stuck her entire head out the window.

"You are going north, aren't you?" Cooper asked as he pointed in the opposite direction of where Brownsville should be.

"We were, but we were about to turn around."

Without thinking or hesitating, Cooper walked toward the car, opened the door, and squeezed in the tiny back seat. The elderly couple never asked where he was going or questioned anything. They just turned the car around and headed toward Brownsville. He never asked them their names either.

They talked a little about the hot and sticky weather. He learned that they were bird watchers and they visited the area multiple times a year. They started talking about specific birds and some rare type they had spotted twelve years ago. They traveled to south Texas every year in hopes of seeing it once again.

Cooper zoned out and barely heard anything they were saying. *What am I doing? What if my lawyer or the court tries to contact me? What if Angel calls?*

"Do you want to go to Whataburger?"

"Huh?" Cooper startled from his deep thoughts. He had almost convinced himself he was on a foolish journey.

"Do you want to go to Whataburger?" the man driving asked again.

"Yes." Cooper paused. "Did I, uh, say anything about Whataburger when I got in the car?"

"No, but we knew you had a meeting and needed to get there," the lady piped up as she turned her head to look at Cooper in the backseat. Then she gave a sly smile and nodded to the man driving as if to say, "I told you so."

Cooper did not know for sure, but he guessed there was more than one Whataburger in the Brownsville area, and his instructions did not even tell him which restaurant.

Do you trust me?

Who or what am I trusting?

The elderly man wheeled his car into the parking lot of a Whataburger. He turned around and handed Cooper a twenty-dollar bill. "Here, you will need this. Get yourself a burger."

"Are you two coming in?" Cooper asked as he opened the car door to step out. Not that he really wanted to spend more time with them.

"Nope, we have to get back to South Padre to spy on some birds," the woman said as she held up her binoculars. "You have a great trip, and we hope you find what you are looking for."

The tires screeched as the Mini Cooper did what looked like an impossible U-turn in the crowded parking lot. He smiled when he read the license plate — 2birdies. An elderly couple that drove a Mini Cooper. *Am I placing my trust in a comedian?* The car made a quick left on the main road and headed back the same direction it had just come from. Cooper chuckled as he considered the irony of a Mini Cooper being the first step on his journey south. He thought he should be laughing hysterically, but crying may have been more appropriate.

"I wonder if they just drove all the way from South Padre to drop me off here?" Cooper whispered. Then he realized he was standing in the middle of a busy parking lot holding a twenty-dollar bill. He tucked the bill in his pocket and turned to enter the restaurant. The only thing he had put in his stomach all day was the over-priced Pabst Blue Ribbon, and he was ready to eat.

When he opened the door, the number of people in the restaurant surprised him. He had left his watch with his other possessions, but he guessed it was almost three o'clock in the afternoon. The lunch crowd should have passed through a few hours ago, but every table was full plus five people in queue at the counter. After waiting his turn, Cooper ordered a double burger with everything on it and some fries. He skipped the Diet Coke in favor of water. Since the rest of his life had been upended and shaken, he thought this may be a good time to give up the diet sodas he had been drinking for the last ten years.

He turned around after getting his tray and scanned the restaurant for a seat. He spotted only one seat open in the entire restaurant. It was next to a family of five. He considered going outside and trying his luck, but took a deep breath and walked toward the empty seat. He made eye contact with a man he presumed was the father, and the man pointed to the seat for him to sit down. About halfway through inhaling his burger, Cooper began thinking his adventure was coming to an abrupt end at a fast food restaurant.

"Do you need a ride across the border into Mexico?"

Cooper froze while chewing a bite of burger that was much larger than he should have had in his mouth. He slowly looked at the brown-eyed girl sitting across from him. Her head bobbed up and down as if to say "you need to say yes." Cooper turned to the parents who also seemed to be nodding "yes." Without thinking, Cooper nodded, and the parents and young girl all grinned at him.

"My name is Carmen. We can help you," said the young girl as she continued to smile, and her father nodded in agreement.

A short time later, he sandwiched himself in the back seat of a Honda Accord with two boys and the young brown-eyed girl on their way to the Mexican border. He had no passport, no identification, and about ten dollars in his pocket. This did not seem like a story that would have a happy ending.

Cooper had heard that the border could be a difficult barrier to cross. But his gated community in Houston was tougher to get into than Mexico. Or at least it seemed to be. The driver of the Honda barely stopped at the checkpoint as he waved and the officer waved back. Cooper did not realize until the car was almost a mile into Mexico that he was slumped down in the backseat lower than all three children.

They darted their way through the streets of the Mexican border town that started with an M that he could never remember the name of. He wanted to call it Metamorphosis, but he knew that wasn't right. They finally arrived at a small home, and Carmen announced, "We're here."

The home was tiny, but neat and well-kept. The two boys went in the front door and right out the back to play in the small fenced backyard. Carmen grabbed Cooper's hand and led him to the sofa. She pointed for him to sit down and then ran down the hall. When she came back, she had a stack of books.

"Can you read to me?" she asked as her brown eyes looked up at him and grew in size as she stared at him.

Cooper was not sure where he was or what he was doing. He had no idea what the next few days would hold for him. He realized that the unknown scared him and that he was not comfortable being this out of control in his life. But those brown eyes staring at him did not care about any of the unsettled emotions rolling around inside him.

He gave his best nervous smile to her and nodded yes. She put the stack of books on his lap and jumped up on the sofa beside him. Cooper read two of the books without a pause.

"Does anyone else in your family speak English?" he asked.

"Some speak a little, but I speak better than they do," she replied. "Don't be afraid, Mama will feed you a yummy meal tonight. You can sleep here, and tomorrow Papa will take you to catch your bus. If you are scared, I can ride with Papa to the bus station."

Cooper stared at Carmen wondering if she was just incredibly perceptive or if she was reading his mind. Or did she know more about his story than he knew?

He took a deep breath and tried to muster a smile. "Thank you for letting me know that. I might be more afraid than I would like to admit."

"It will all be okay. You can trust me."

She knew her stuff.

By midmorning the next day, he was on a bus heading south. Carmen's father had paid the ticket and handed Cooper some

Mexican currency. He walked Cooper to the bus and spoke to the bus driver in a loud demonstrative tone before he let Cooper board.

Cooper sat toward the middle of the bus and realized he was waving to Carmen and her papa as the bus was pulling away. He found himself whispering, "It will all be okay. It will all be okay."

Cooper had trouble remembering exactly how he arrived in the bed he was currently in after leaving Metamorphosis, Mexico. Or whatever the name of that town was. The rest of the journey south was a blur. He recalled bouncing up and down on a bus for at least three days. The trip was slow because of the many stops along the way.

He changed buses once in San Salvador. His bus had stopped at a terminal, and after everyone exited, the bus driver walked back to Cooper and touched his arm as if to say "follow me." The driver, whose name badge said "Jesus," led Cooper behind a long line of parked buses.

The driver knocked on a bus that had its door closed. The door opened, and a man sitting in the driver's seat motioned for Cooper to step in. He pointed to the bus seats, and Cooper stepped into the aisle and went about halfway back before taking a seat. Twenty minutes later the driver started the bus and drove through the lot to a stand with a group of people waiting under an awning. Luggage was loaded, and the people filed onto the bus.

His lack of sleep and failure to eat must have zapped his immune system because he started feeling hot then cold in waves shortly after the bus left San Salvador. At times it felt almost as if his brain were cooking. He could barely keep his head up and kept drifting in and out of a dreamlike state.

Cooper knew that he had to have passed through multiple national borders, but he never recalled being asked for documents or identification. He thought that everyone was asked to leave the bus at least once, but he stayed in his seat. He went into a deep sleep only to wake up hours later with the bus bouncing down the highway.

He also remembered being helped from the bus and carried to a truck with a camper-type shell on the back. The people helping him were speaking Spanish, and they laid him on a mat in the camper. That was the last thing Cooper remembered until he saw the face of the bearded man.

Did I make it to Costa Rica? How long have I been out of it? Am I in the location that's my destination? Or my destiny? Did the bearded man bring me here?

Cooper finally mustered the energy to sit up in bed. He felt weak, but his stomach growled for ten seconds as if to say, "Hey, we need some food down here."

The room he was in was modern and bright. If he was in some Central American country, this place had many of the amenities of an American resort. Soft sheets and a fluffy comforter. The queen-sized bed faced a wall that was all glass. The window treatments were simple but what many would consider understated elegance. The sliding door was opened slightly, and a cool breeze blew the curtains back and forth in a soft cadence.

Cooper stood up. His legs felt wobbly, and he plopped back down on the bed. He took a deep breath and tried again. This time he paused as he stood just to make sure he was going to stay steady.

He guessed that the door to the left of the bed was the bathroom. He only wobbled once as he slid his bare feet across the chilly tile floor. A big walk-in shower, a toilet, and double sinks on the vanity were beyond what he was expecting.

Cooper stared in the mirror above the vanity. He did not like what he saw. His face looked pale and drawn. His skin was pasty white. And while most of his body was skinny and almost frail, his belly had that spare tire look that men joke about. He once thought he was strong and fit, almost invincible, and at least moderately good looking. There was nothing strong about what he saw in the mirror. He was a mess. Physically, mentally, and just about any other way one could evaluate him.

He was wearing his Hang Loose t-shirt and the same boxer briefs he had put on when he left South Padre. *How many days...or weeks...ago was that? The bus trip was at least three days, but it seems like weeks since I left Padre Island.*

He tried not to think about someone undressing him, but it did cause him a bit of unease.

A new toothbrush, toothpaste, razor, and other toiletries were lying on the vanity countertop as if they had been placed there by a hotel maid.

He wanted to grab the toothbrush and start getting the crud off of his teeth and out of his mouth. But the door over his left shoulder caught his eye. He spun around a little too quickly and felt another little wobble. Cooper paused to catch his breath again before walking over to the door.

He opened the door, and as he did, a light automatically went on. A bench against the wall held some neatly folded clothes. As he stepped over to the bench, he recognized the clothes as the ones he had put on when he left South Padre. They had been laundered and pressed, and *The Tablet* rested on top of the pile. On the opposite side of the closet, clothes hung from a rod—a few pairs of khaki pants, shirts, plus a pair of shoes on the floor.

Cooper studied the clothes on the rod briefly before stepping closer to look at the sizes. He checked the shirts, then the pants, then the shoes. He slowly stepped backward and stared at the clothes. They were all his exact sizes.

His mind raced back to a sentence in the instructions he had been given: *Take nothing for your journey.*

9

Everything was green. Dark green. All shades of green. Green as far as the eye could see. Cooper stood on the veranda off of the bedroom gazing down the hill at the mountainous area in the distance. The shower he had just finished was the most enjoyable he could remember. He had stood under the water for at least thirty minutes. He shaved and then put on clothes that fit his broken down body perfectly.

But he was still not sure where he was.

Or more importantly why he was here.

He walked back inside the bedroom and through the door leading to a hallway. The short hall turned to the left as he exited the bedroom, went past a door that appeared to be the main entrance, and then opened up into a large gathering room. He walked slowly and cautiously, almost expecting someone to jump out and surprise him, or to at least run into another person.

A weak "Hello, anyone here?" crackled from his lips. No answer.

He looked around the expansive room. A large island surrounded by stools separated the living space from a modern kitchen. He crossed the room and discovered another bedroom directly opposite from his. It had the same views that he had seen from his bedroom. So far, from what he could tell, the villa was basically a large gathering room sandwiched by two bedrooms. A covered veranda ran along the backside of the villa and was accessible by large glass doors from both bedrooms and the gathering room.

Cooper wandered back to the kitchen and looked around. He needed some food and coffee. Maybe not in that order. Unsure of whether he should start scavenging through the cabinets or if he needed to wait, he walked back to the large glass door leading out to the veranda. He spotted a table under the awning, and his stomach rumbled at the sight of a covered tray on the table. He did not run to the table, but he realized he was moving quickly. Maybe too quickly for his weak legs. When he reached the table, he picked up the tray lid, and a big smile spread across his face as he inhaled the aromas of a beautiful spread of food.

He paused and looked up. He spun around once just to make sure he was the only one around. Even though he didn't spot anyone, clearly he was not alone. Room service does not appear out of thin air. At least not in the world he was from.

He quickly pulled out the chair and sat down. His refined upbringing seemed to escape him as he grabbed a fork and attacked the food. It was still warm so it must have been placed here just a few minutes before he stepped outside.

Either the food was really delicious, or he was ravenous. Maybe a little bit of both. He was not exactly sure what he was eating, but he ate like a dog licks its food bowl. He recognized some rice and also flavors of peppers, beans, and maybe some bacon or pork. Two fried eggs, sliced avocado, and what looked like a soft taco were also on the plate.

He inhaled about twelve bites before he paused to raise his head and notice his surroundings.

From what he could see, the house where he sat was at the highest point and there was a gradual slope down to a hedge at the lower end of the property. The small estate had to be at least a football field in length. The tall hedge surrounded everything Cooper could see and it appeared to serve as a fence.

Was the hedge to keep people out? Or is it to keep people like me inside?

His best guess was he was in a small compound. It was nice. It was clean. And he was eating good food. He shrugged his shoulders as if to say "who cares if I am trapped here."

He could not see what was immediately on the other side of the hedge, but the terrain continued sloping downward until it began rising again to a lush green hillside covered with trees. The opposite slope was steeper and rose to a point slightly higher than where Cooper sat. Other hills surrounded the one across from him, and mountains lined the horizon for as far as he could see.

The sky was as blue as the sky could have been. Scattered white puffy clouds dotted it like someone had drawn fluffy pieces of cotton against a light blue canvas. Based on the shadows on the ground, he knew the sun was at his back, and he assumed he was facing west as he looked out over the hills and small mountains in the distance.

When his eating slowed to a more civilized pace, Cooper took in more of his surroundings. If being a fugitive was in his future, there were many places that would have been more unpleasant than this place. His stomach finally felt full after days of being empty. He looked down at his clean plate. Only one thing was missing.

Coffee.

"How long has it been since I really enjoyed a good cup of coffee?" he asked himself.

He missed his espresso machine in his office. *Maybe this sickness is related to lack of coffee.*

At this point, TR's Mr. Coffee machine would have been acceptable. Cooper laughed to himself thinking that Folger's might even satisfy his craving.

He looked up from his empty plate and noticed a puff of smoke rising above the hedge at the end of the property. As he was staring, the smoke became thicker, and he spotted a small chimney pipe barely visible above the hedge.

Cooper stood up and pushed away from the table. He stepped off the veranda and slowly walked down a path that led toward the smoke. For some reason, he felt drawn to the smoke like it was a giant magnet. He could not stop walking down the hill, nor did he want to stop. His heart raced. His palms got sweaty. And he kept walking.

As he approached the hedge, he discovered a small cottage on the other side. The small structure was wedged into the farthest corner of the compound. And it was surrounded by hedges on three sides. He glanced back up the hill towards the main house. The architecture of the cottage was noticeably different.

The cottage just did not fit in.

Cooper paused. After his slow journey down the hill, his feet were now planted as he stared at the door. Something magnetic was pulling him, but his feet would not move now that he was here. He knew he wanted to go in, but he wasn't sure what to expect. He raised his hand to tap on the wooden door.

Just as his hand was about to make contact with the wooden door, it swung wide open. Cooper was face to face with the bearded man.

COACH

"Mr. Travis. Welcome. We have been expecting you."

10

Life is made up of many moments that combine to create our journey. That journey also includes forks and crossroads where decisions must be made to turn left or turn right or stop and stand still. Cooper's current journey had brought him to a cottage that looked as if it were dropped into a villa in Costa Rica from another place and possibly another time. Nothing made sense about where he was or why he was here.

Now Cooper Travis stood at the door of that cottage with the bearded man directly in front of him inviting him in. Any fear or hesitation that was controlling him subsided for a brief moment. A moment long enough for him to take the next step in his journey.

If the exterior of the cabin was dated compared to the surrounding architecture, then the interior of the cottage was like stepping back in time. The cottage was small with no modern lights and no outside light visible. A fire burned in the fireplace, and its light and warmth filled the place with heat and a glow. Two rockers and a small table stood in the middle of the cottage facing the fireplace. A countertop to Cooper's right appeared to serve as the kitchen area. A small opening to his left had a double curtain over it. Since there was no bed in the main room, Cooper assumed the bedroom was behind the curtain.

"I thought you might want some coffee, Mr. Travis. I have been preparing some in anticipation of your visit."

"I would love some coffee," Cooper responded. "In fact, I was thinking that coffee may just be what I really need at this time."

"You require more than just coffee, but we will allow that to be our starting point."

Cooper noticed a kettle hanging on a hook in the fireplace. It must've been what the bearded man was using to boil water.

As Cooper continued to scan the room, he realized there were no lamps, no microwave, no oven, no TV — nothing that used electricity at all.

"It will only take me a few minutes to prepare our coffee," the man said.

"Can I ask you a question? Who are you and where am I?" Cooper said with somewhat of a sheepish tone.

"Great question. First of all, my name is Asa Jordan, and I've been looking forward to meeting you. Please call me Asa. And as to where you are, welcome to Costa Rica." Asa pointed to one of the rockers facing the fireplace. "Please have a seat, Mr. Travis."

Cooper sat down and felt the warmth coming from the fire. For some reason, he was not uncomfortable with this person named Asa who had been waiting for him in a country that he had never visited. In fact, it was almost the opposite feeling. He was relaxed and comfortable, an unusual feeling but one he could get used to.

"It seems as if your journey to Costa Rica may have been a challenge. It's a tough trip to make even if you're feeling well. When one is sick, I am sure it can be very difficult," Asa said.

Not knowing exactly what to say, Cooper nodded in response and fought the urge to drill Asa with questions. His mind raced, and he felt his impatience building. But deep inside, he felt calm. The more he thought of questions, the more his soul took over and made him relax, stay quiet, and breathe. As he sat in front of the fire, he bounced between taking deep breaths and not breathing at all. After a few moments, he decided to just sit and rock and try to breathe.

Cooper shifted in his seat to watch Asa at the kitchen counter. Two mugs sat on the counter, and Asa held two small bags that appeared to have coffee beans in them. Cooper watched as Asa placed one bag in a bowl and pressed it with a short stubby ceramic stick. Then he laid the bag on the counter and pressed it with a rectangular piece of metal. He picked up the bag and caressed its contents for a few moments. Then he repeated the entire process over and over for the first bag before starting on the second bag.

Cooper wanted to ask if he was manually grinding coffee beans, but he decided to just sit and watch as he rocked. The creaking of the rocking chair was the loudest sound in the cottage until a loud bubbling hiss came from the fireplace as the water heated to a boil.

"Would you get that kettle and bring it to me please?" Asa asked. "And make sure you use the mitt."

Cooper stood and walked to the fireplace. An old mitt rested on the rod that extended into the fire and held the kettle over the flame. Cooper put the mitt on his hand and slowly pulled the kettle away from the flame. He reached down, grabbed the kettle, and walked carefully over to the counter as the water rolled and churned inside.

As excited as Cooper was to get a fresh cup of coffee, what he saw made him wonder what he was about to drink. The small bags Asa had worked on now rested over each mug. Asa looked up from the mugs, took the kettle from Cooper, and poured the hot water slowly over the coffee grounds. Cooper watched bubbles form on the cloth bags as the hot water hit the grounds before dripping into the mugs. As one that called himself a coffee snob, he had never seen coffee prepared this way.

What is this going to taste like? Surely it won't be anything like TR's coffee. He smiled as he thought about the modern coffee culture learning about this method and opening coffee shops all over touting it as "the best coffee ever."

"Now we wait," Asa said. "Let's have a seat."

The two men walked over to the rockers. Cooper sat down again in the rocker to the left of the fireplace while Asa sat in the one to the right.

"We have about ten minutes, Mr. Travis. Let's get to know each other."

Cooper wanted to know a few things, and he didn't feel very patient, so he bluntly asked, "Did I see you at the bar on South Padre Island?"

"I have been watching you for some time, Mr. Travis. It is possible that you could have seen me in many places. But do not be alarmed, as you will see the more time we spend together, our relationship is for a purpose."

Asa's answer didn't alarm him, but Cooper realized he once again did not have a response. Instead, for the first time since he had been in the cottage, he looked straight at Asa's face. The man's skin was dark, but Cooper could not determine if that was because of his nationality or because he had spent considerable time out in the sun. His face was surrounded by a full head of hair that was more gray than dark. His beard was the same—gray and full with specks of black throughout. He could've been in his forties or even his mid to late eighties. Cooper really couldn't tell. He remembered as they were standing next to each other that Asa seemed neither tall nor short. In fact, it was almost as if he was the exact same height as Cooper, about six feet tall.

Cooper scanned downward from his head and noted his clothing. He had never seen someone dressed this way, yet it seemed as if he was entirely comfortable with what he wore. His light blue shirt was a linen or soft cotton and could have been a work shirt or dress shirt. He wore a sports coat that was a blend between a black and gray. Just like the shirt, this sport coat seemed to be clothing that could be worn in a business setting or for something more casual. His tan khaki pants fell over well-worn leather work boots. The outfit's style reminded Cooper of Indiana Jones without the fedora hat and the whip. And the leather jacket was replaced with an informal sport coat.

His scan had only taken a few seconds, but when he looked back up at Asa's face, what he saw next caused a warmth beyond what was coming from the fire to fill Cooper's entire body.

A few days ago, as his body had raged with fever, Cooper had looked into Asa's eyes when he was twelve inches from him. Today, he was drawn to his eyes again as they sat and waited for the coffee. He had never seen eyes as bright blue as Asa's. He wasn't sure if the light from the fire caused the brightness of the blue or if they were just a unique color. However, more than the color captivated Cooper. As he looked straight into Asa's eyes, it seemed as if they had a depth that went on for forever. It was as if the eyes were a water puddle of blue that was as deep as an ocean.

Cooper continued to stare, and Asa returned his gaze for ten seconds at least. He did not know how to describe what he saw in the eyes, but the only word that came to mind was tranquility.

The feeling that Asa's eyes inspired gave Cooper the courage to ask the question that needed to be answered more than any other.

"Why am I here?" Cooper finally asked. He really wanted to know how he got to where he currently was, but he knew finding out why was more important.

"Why do you think you are here, Mr. Travis?"

"I guess it would be best to say that I have made a mess of my life. And I am not really sure what will happen in the near future. All I know is that, more than any time in my life, it would be wise for me to admit that I am a failure."

"Are you willing to admit you may need to redefine your life? Redefine success as culture and society has defined it? Are you ready to make some changes? " Asa moved the conversation forward without directly responding to what Cooper said.

"I guess that I am." Cooper shrugged as he considered Asa's deep questions. "I'm not even sure what that looks like or if I am able to fix the mess I'm in."

"Well then, you're exactly where you need to be at the perfect time." Asa smiled as he responded. "Are you ready for some coffee?"

The men stood and walked back to the counter where Cooper watched as Asa removed the bag of beans from the mug and let it continue dripping for a few seconds. He then handed Cooper the mug and repeated the process with the second cup. Cooper paused for a moment. He did not want to be rude to his host, but it was very obvious that black coffee was the only option.

Asa picked up his cup and walked back over to the rockers. After sitting down, Cooper waited for Asa to take the first sip, not really out of politeness or respect, but mostly just wanting to see Asa's facial expression when he took a drink.

Asa wrapped both hands loosely around his cup and pulled it to his nose. His eyes closed as he took a deep breath to inhale the aroma of the coffee. He pressed the mug to his lips and sipped as he tilted the cup. He was obviously not in a rush. With his eyes still closed, he took a long slow sip and then pulled the cup away from his face. He opened his eyes and looked over toward Cooper.

"Excellent," he whispered.

Cooper took this as his cue to take a sip. He was comforted that Asa did not gag or cough after taking his first drink. He did not duplicate the long slow inhale and sip that Asa had displayed, but he did pause to enjoy the smell for longer than he had anticipated.

That first sip of coffee was unlike anything Cooper had ever experienced as a coffee connoisseur. The flavor started mild but seemed to build strength as it went down. The most unique feature was the hint of something sweet. Most coffee has a bitterness, and many seem to think that the best coffee has an acidic bitter taste. This cup almost tasted like it had sweetener added. But Cooper had watched every step of the simple process and knew that ground coffee beans and hot water were the only ingredients..

At first, Cooper wondered if he was just dealing with coffee withdrawal after not having any for a few weeks. But the more he sipped that morning, the better it got. And any coffee drinker knows that is not usually the case. Even the best coffee can taste horrible when you get to the last cooled off sip at the bottom of the cup.

Cooper thought that he had tasted all the best coffees in the world, and he had been confident that the cup of coffee in his hands would never compare to those. Now he questioned what he knew about coffee because Asa's coffee was the opposite of everything the coffee world expected. Simple was the best word to describe it. Cooper had to admit that it was the best cup of coffee he had ever experienced.

Only later would he learn Asa's secret..

11

The next few weeks were a struggle for Cooper. He was disappointed that his conversation with Asa ended with just a cup of coffee and nothing more than introductions. Asa had mentioned that he would be in and out over the next few weeks. He did not give Cooper any details other than saying something about a special project that needed his attention. Asa encouraged Cooper to rest and meditate on the question, "Why am I here?" He said the two of them would speak again soon.

While Cooper knew that he should enjoy the easy pace and the days that passed with absolutely nothing for him to do, he discovered that being disconnected from the world and not thinking about appointments or a "to do" list ate away at his self-worth. He had been working nonstop for as long as he could remember and was wired to believe that he could fix things and that he could do it quickly. The time in Costa Rica moved at such a slow pace that it almost drove him crazy. It was even slower than the few weeks in South Padre. He was continually reminded of how challenging it was to rest and do nothing.

One thing that Cooper definitely missed while Asa was away was his coffee. For some reason, no coffee was served in the main house. Asa's cottage not only held Cooper's future within its walls, but it was currently the only place that he could get his coffee fix. The longer he waited for his second visit to the cottage, the more he desired the coffee.

Cooper had stayed in some nice resorts and five-star hotels all over the world. His current accommodations would not qualify as a five-star resort, but the peaceful surroundings were immaculately cleaned and maintained. And the food and service were excellent. Food magically appeared, and the villa was cleaned in a miraculous way. The word "miraculous" is what Cooper used to describe the service because he never saw anyone performing the tasks. It just happened.

Out of boredom, Cooper decided to explore the villa and the surrounding area. He found three bicycles in the garage barn that was on the property. The bikes were old school with only one gear. He could not remember when he had last ridden a bike, especially a classic single speed, but that didn't stop him from attempting to ride.

His first few rides were depressing. They only reminded him how out of shape and neglected his body really was. When exiting the front of the villa, the road went up a steep hill to the left and sloped downward to the right. He attempted the uphill grade once and found that he was able to barely get out of sight of the villa before he was off the bike and pushing. Fortunately for him, the road ended shortly after he began.

He also attempted the ride down the hill, but it became so steep and winding that he became concerned that he would not be able to get back up.

While he thought he would enjoy the adventure of riding a bike, his self image started to take a beating because, even after a few rides, he could not get more than a mile from the villa. He decided the next best thing would be exploring on foot inside the villa walls. The wall around the villa was ten feet tall in most places and appeared to be a thick hedge, but upon further inspection, Cooper realized the hedge covered a block wall. At the back of the villa property, he discovered a double gate door that had some vines and vegetation covering portions of it. It was difficult to tell if the gate had been opened recently or if it had not been touched for years.

Cooper avoided the vine-covered gate for the first week after he discovered it. Instead, he walked around the property and occasionally ventured out the front gate, which was wide enough for two or three vehicles to pass through at once. The vine-covered gate at the back of the property was barely wide enough for one small vehicle to go through if both doors of the gate were open.

The following week, Cooper stopped to stare at the vine-covered gate for a few minutes. The doors curved at the top to match an arch that extended over the top of the wall. On the door on the left side, he noticed an odd feature—hinges and a small knob. He brushed away some of the vegetation and found a narrow door no more than three feet tall inside the larger door. The small door looked like one that would be at the entrance of a treehouse or a children's play area.

Cooper was intrigued by the small door and what was on the other side, but most days he just walked on by and never thought about it. A few times he stopped to give the door a push, but it seemed as if it had not been opened in some time. He looked around for a handle or a latch or a lock holding the door closed, but couldn't find one. He even gave it a good shove and a strong pull. Nothing.

One day, he paused longer than usual to stare at the gate. Something was different. He ran his fingers along the edge of the small door. It was pushed in slightly. Cooper gave it a light shove with his hand and watched as it swung open away from the villa.

He stooped down to look through the short and narrow opening. On the other side was a lush, green jungle with a path running down the middle of the forest. Cooper squeezed through the small door and stood up straight on the outside of the gate. He looked to his right and left and noted how the jungle seemed to attach itself to the hedge and block wall surrounding the property. In fact, the jungle and the hedge seemed to be one and the same making it impossible to walk along the outer edge of the wall.

Days earlier while standing on the veranda, he had noticed a gradual slope down into a valley with a small mountain on the other side. From where he stood now, he could not see any of those features, only the trail in front of him cutting through the green forest.

He briefly hesitated before whispering, "What do I have to lose?"

He started walking at a brisk pace down the tree-lined path. After a few minutes, he heard the faint sound of running water. He picked up his pace as he anticipated what he might discover. He was not sure how far from the back gate of the villa he had walked, but the sound of water became louder and louder the farther he traveled.

The trail opened up as it met a river and then veered left to follow along the shore. Cooper wasn't sure if "river" was the right word to describe what he was looking at. It was somewhere between a creek and a river, and the water flowing in it was clean and crisp like one would envision in a mountain stream.

The path continued its gradual descent, which was not very steep at all but just enough that Cooper noticed it. He glanced at the water often and became curious about what was on the other side. There is something about a mountain that cries out to be climbed. And rivers beg to be crossed so that mysteries on the other side can be discovered. Unfortunately, he did not see any areas that were narrow or even shallow enough for him to cross.

He had been walking for about fifteen minutes when he spotted a bridge in the distance. Cooper's heart raced a bit as if he had discovered a buried treasure or a hidden cave. When he reached the bridge, he realized the main trail continued straight ahead while another trail split to his right crossing over the bridge.

Cooper walked to the bridge and paused in the middle. He looked back up the river, which seemed to stretch as far as he could see and then disappear. He turned around to look downstream and noticed the same thing—clean flowing water as far as he could see.

While standing in the middle of the bridge, he inhaled long, deep breaths to let the surroundings fill his body. He heard birds chirping, but couldn't actually see any. A low rumble sound bounced all over the area as running water cascaded over the rocks. The sun was high overhead and brought warmth to Cooper while a coolness rose up from the water. It was the perfect balance of warm and cold.

He studied the opposite side of the bridge and briefly considered exploring some more. The trail continued for a bit along the other side of the shore, but then made its way gradually up the hill he had seen from the veranda. He decided he had ventured far enough away from the villa for the day and turned to make his way back.

As Cooper stooped to go through the narrow door to enter the villa property, he felt the urge to speak to Asa. Asa had told him that he had to leave for a few weeks, but Cooper decided to knock on the door of the cottage just to see if he had returned. He stood up from stooping through the gate, looked to his right, and walked the short distance to the cottage.

He stopped at the door and knocked. No sound. Nothing. He knocked again and waited.

He realized impatience was bubbling up inside him. The great Cooper Travis was not accustomed to waiting on anyone. The world had waited on him. But here he was in a strange country in the middle of nowhere getting anxious about meeting with an old man that he really knew nothing about.

He let out a heavy sigh. Not a relaxed, peaceful sigh but rather a sarcastic sigh that said "What the heck am I doing here?"

He stepped away from the door to inspect the cottage. It was not as big as he had thought when he was inside. The outside was stone all around. He looked up. The thatched roof was not more than fifteen feet tall at its highest point. He walked around the side of the cottage on a path barely wide enough for him to fit between the interior hedge and the outside wall. The backside of the cottage and one side wall were almost attached to the outside hedge that surrounded the villa. Other than the path he was walking on, Cooper could not see anything between the hedge and the outside cottage walls on the two sides. It was as if the hedge and cottage had grown together over the years.

The cottage had obviously been there for a long time. In fact, the cottage appeared to be older than the other buildings. And the style was different. It was like someone had dropped an old English countryside cottage in the middle of a Costa Rican villa.

As he stepped back to the front of the cottage, Cooper noticed something strange. The cottage had no windows.

12

Most days were filled with rain or the threat of rain. Whenever the rain poured down, Cooper sat on the back veranda of the villa and watched. On the few days that were clear, he walked down the path and continued exploring past the bridge that crossed the creek. Every day he walked a little farther than the previous.

His first trip down the path had caused both exhilaration and nervousness. Exhilaration because he was doing something instead of just sitting and watching the rain. Nervousness because he was a stranger in a country where he did not speak the language and he had no money.

His desire to get up and move and do something gave him the courage to overcome his nervousness, and he continued exploring. He discovered that, if he did not cross the bridge, the dirt trail continued along the river. Cooper rarely walked fast, but the excitement of discovering something new always caused the pace of his breathing to increase whenever he passed the point where he had turned around on his previous trip.

Today, he had been walking for about an hour when he heard the faint sound of traffic in the distance. Curious, he kept walking. He rounded a bend and discovered that the villa trail ended on a dirt road. Since the day was clear with no clouds and no threat of rain, he ventured down the dirt road. He passed a few small houses before the dirt road also came to an end. He stopped at the corner of the dirt road and a paved road that must have been a main thoroughfare because a car buzzed by every ten to fifteen seconds.

Not sure which way to go, Cooper looked to his right. The road ran past a cemetery, and in the distance, he could see a cluster of buildings and houses. To his left were a few scattered houses, and it was obviously the direction that carried people away from the town. Across the paved road was a large green field with picnic tables randomly scattered around.

Cooper looked right. Then he looked left.

I think I should just visit the park.

He waited for a small car to pass by before trotting across the road. As he reached the entrance to the park, he heard yelling and whistles off in the distance. Cooper walked toward the activity just like a bug is drawn to light on a hot summer night. His days had been so slow and boring that almost anything would be exciting to him.

On the other side of the park's grass field, he spotted chain-link fences separating multiple playing areas. On each field, groups of kids were running around kicking a soccer ball. Cooper moved toward the field with the most noise and the oldest group of athletes.

A rickety set of bleachers sat just outside the chain-link fence surrounding the field. Cooper eased onto the bleachers to pass some time and watch the local sport. The group of young men on the field appeared to be middle school age. He guessed they were practicing or playing a scrimmage match since there were no formal uniforms or referees. He knew very little about the strategy of soccer, so he just watched as the ball went to his right followed by a group of players. Then the ball went to the left, and the group moved left.

Cooper spotted two coaches standing on the opposite side of the field. One stayed quiet, but the other was red-faced and constantly yelling at the top of his lungs. And whenever he took a break from yelling, he blew his whistle. Periodically, everyone on the field stopped and stared at the coach as he yelled instructions or correction.

"Just like my old coach. I wish I knew Spanish. I'd probably be learning some profanity," Cooper whispered to himself as he thought back to his experiences with TR and Coach when he was a similar age to the teenaged athletes.

A few seconds later, one of the players lagged behind the mass of bodies following the ball to Cooper's right. The coach whistled for everyone to stop, and he sprinted toward the player that was lagging. The coach stopped in front of the player with his face only inches away from the boy. The explosion that followed could have been measured on a Richter scale. The yelling lasted for only a few seconds, but it was as if everything moved in slow motion and the tirade went on and on and on. The coach then circled the player while pointing down toward the rest of the team. By the time the coach eased up, the boy's head had drooped until he was looking down at his feet.

Cooper continued watching as the coach asked what sounded like a question and the player slowly nodded. The coach repeated the question with more emphasis and the player nodded with more energy. The coach turned and pointed toward the team, and the player sprinted to connect with the others.

"Yep, just like Coach. Even if you don't have the most skill, you can at least hustle and put forth maximum effort." Cooper smiled at the memory and how well that lesson had served him over the years.

The next ten minutes of the scrimmage were fun for Cooper to watch. The coach went silent, and the player who had been the focus of his wrath ran up and down the field in perpetual motion and was the first one to the ball almost every time. Cooper still had no idea what the strategy of the sport was, but he knew that one player was now out hustling every other player.

A loud whistle signaled the end of the practice. The coach and his quiet assistant walked to the middle of the field where all the players circled around them. Both shared with the team in a more conversational tone.

Cooper looked over to the west and noticed the sun beginning to touch the trees. *I need to get going before it gets dark. I'm still at least an hour's walk from the villa.*

He stepped off the bleachers and started to turn away from the field when something caught his eye. The team huddle had broken up, and the players were running toward a building off in the distance. One player and the coach remained at center field.

Cooper paused to watch what would happen next. *I wonder if the coach is going to let him have it again.*

What happened next proved Cooper wrong.

The coach stooped down on one knee and looked up at the young player. If the conversation ten minutes ago was an explosion, this exchange was as soft as a baby's whisper. The coach looked straight into the eyes of the player, and as he spoke, the posture of the boy became more and more erect. After more conversation, the coach stood and gave the boy a big, long hug. The coach put his arm over the boy's shoulder, and they walked off the field together.

Cooper stared at the pair in the distance for a moment before walking at a brisk pace across the park and down the dirt road. As soon as he reached the path to the villa, his mind attempted to process what he had just witnessed.

I guess there are times when we need a kick in the butt. And times we need a hug. All I remember Coach giving us were the kicks. But maybe I just missed the times he gave hugs.

After ducking through the small door inside the gate at the back of the villa property, he glanced toward Asa's cottage. *I wonder if Asa is going to kick my butt or if he will give me a hug? I'm not even sure I know which one I really need right now.*

He passed by the cottage and continued the short walk up to the main house as the sun disappeared behind his back. He entered the house through the glass door off of the veranda and immediately noticed that the door on the back side of the kitchen was cracked open slightly. That door had been closed and locked since the first day he had explored the house. He had attempted to open it a few times and assumed the property owners used whatever was behind the door as a storage closet. Now, if the door was open, that meant someone had been in the house while he was gone.

Curious, and slightly concerned for his own safety, he tiptoed across the stone floor and peeked through the crack like a cat. He slowly pushed the door open and discovered a short, dark-haired woman with her head down carrying a handful of items as she glided toward him.

When she glanced up, she screamed and threw the items at his face. Fortunately, for Cooper, it was just some sheets and a few towels. But the sheer force of the throw caused him to stumble backward out of the doorway and into the kitchen. He would have most likely fallen flat on his back if not for bumping into the kitchen island.

After the screaming was done and Cooper had righted himself against the island, he realized he was staring directly at his mysterious cleaning and cooking fairy. But she was obviously not a fairy, even though she was no taller than five foot tall. She stared at Cooper with what might have been the biggest eyes he had ever seen. They may have been enlarged because he had just scared her, or maybe they seemed big because she was so small. Her hair that he had initially thought was dark had started the graying process a few years before.

"I apologize for scaring you. Are you the one that has been doing all the cooking and cleaning here?" Cooper asked.

She slowly nodded and smiled.

"Well, I do want to thank you for your excellent service."

She slowly nodded and smiled.

"And I also apologize if I have made it difficult for you in any way."

She slowly nodded and smiled.

"Do you speak English?" he asked.

She slowly nodded and smiled.

He realized that there may be a communication challenge and he should clarify whether they could truly understand each other. He decided to ask a bizarre question. "Would it be possible for me to have a New York style deep dish pizza every day for lunch?"

She slowly nodded and smiled.

Cooper knew that his questions were not understood, and he knew very little Spanish. He wished he had spent a bit more time learning the language in high school Spanish class.

"Yo hablo Inglés?" Cooper asked. He wondered why he had changed his accent as if to mimic someone speaking Spanish.

She paused. And then she proceeded to launch into a stream of Spanish at a pace way too fast for his skills. She kept going and going and going as Cooper tried to stop her.

When she paused to take a breath, Cooper yelled, "No hable!" He thought he said "I do not speak" but later wondered if he actually told her to stop speaking. And with his tone, he may have told her to shut up. Either way, she stopped.

"No comprendo," he said with hesitation. Maybe his high school Spanish class was going to pay off after all. He just wished he would stop using a cheesy accent every time he spoke.

She slowly nodded and smiled.

"Como se llama?" he asked. Finally, he was able to speak like a normal person and not sound like some Mexican in an old Humphrey Bogart western movie.

"Maria," she replied. She smiled and slowly nodded.

"Me llamo Cooper."

She nodded and smiled.

They stood for a few seconds and then both seemed to realize that they had exhausted their communications skills. Cooper bent down and picked up the towels and sheets off the floor. He handed them to Maria who smiled once again and then stepped back into the room off the kitchen and closed the door.

The Tablet - October

I don't know what the date is. I'm pretty sure it's early October. Maybe around the 10th.

I have no idea why I am here or what the future holds. My lawyer thought my sentencing might happen in September. If it did, well, I am in trouble because no one knows where I am.

I miss my Angel. I hope that she is well and that we can be together again soon.

I want to be patient, but I am ready for something to happen. I am ready to do something. This sitting and waiting is painful to me. Maybe that is something that I need to change. Impatience and a personality that wants to perform at all times is obviously not something that has worked well for me.

I need to be patient.

I need to be able to relax.

I need to change and be the man that Angel needs me to be.

I may need a hug. Or I may need a kick in the pants.

As Cooper contemplated what to write next, if anything, he listened to the rain beating on the porch roof. The rain had begun shortly after his encounter with Maria and it had not stopped for two days. He was studying the hedge wall in the distance when he noticed a spiral of smoke coming from the cottage chimney.

He jumped up to get a better look to make sure his eyes were not playing tricks on him.

"Yes!" he yelled as he tossed *The Tablet* onto the lounge chair. He sprinted down the path, through the small grove of trees, and almost wiped out as he came to a stop at the cottage door.

Without realizing his excitement, he began banging on the door. He waited only a few seconds in the rain for the door to open.

"Mr. Travis, it is so good to see you. Please come in." His host greeted him as if it had only been yesterday since they had seen each other.

13

Cooper immediately felt the familiar warmth as he entered the cottage. The fire was blazing, and while it was not very cold outside, his damp clothes clung to his body causing a slight chill.

"Please, my friend, stand by the fire to warm up. I will bring you a towel," Asa ducked through a curtained doorway and returned seconds later with a towel. "How would you like a cup of coffee?"

"I would love a cup of coffee," Cooper wiped his face with the towel and roughly ran it over his head.

"Then please move the kettle over the fire, Mr. Travis."

Cooper swung the metal arm so that the kettle was over the flame. As he stood in front of the fire, he took the time to observe the interior of the cottage again. The walls were the same stone as the exterior. Wood was stacked almost four feet high on either side of the fireplace. The fireplace was on the wall opposite the main door. Surrounding the door were shelves from floor to ceiling and from one corner to the other. Books packed every square inch of the shelves. The lighting was dim in the cottage, but Cooper could see that most of the books were hardbound and appeared to have some age on them.

To his right was a wall with a double curtain that was not quite closed. Through the gap, he spotted a small single bed no wider than a twin. The other curtained doorway on the same wall must have led to the bathroom because that's where Asa had retrieved the towel from.

Two rocking chairs rested in the center of the room just like the last time he had been inside the cottage. A few candles sat on a round table in between the chairs. The candles and the fire were the only light in the room, but the warmth and the light created an inviting and cozy atmosphere.

A thought crossed Cooper's mind and a quick scan around the cottage confirmed what he wanted to check— no windows.

To his left, Asa worked on the coffee in the kitchen area. He stood behind a long counter that looked more like a table. Underneath the counter were a few items, such as pots and pans, but no one could say it was a fully stocked, modern kitchen. On the end of the counter opposite of where Asa was working and closest to the fire, Cooper noticed a sink, which he had missed during his last visit.

"Do you have running water in here?" Cooper was almost embarrassed that, of all the questions he had thought of over the last few weeks, his first question was so trivial. And it sounded condescending as it came out of his mouth.

"Mr. Travis, I am a simple man that does not require many of the trappings of modern society as you can observe. But I do enjoy running water, and I even have the luxury of a flushable toilet that I have access to," Asa smiled as he tilted his head toward the door on the opposite wall.

Cooper ventured away from the fire and closer to the counter in order to get a better view of how Asa was holding the small bag and pressing the beans between his fingers. "Are you grinding those beans by hand?"

"Not entirely, Mr. Travis. Are my methods strange to you?"

Cooper thought about how he had made most of his coffee in his office machine. Not wanting to risk further embarrassment after the running water question, he chose his words carefully, "I can say that I am not familiar with this technique."

"If you have interest, I can explain my simple process."

Cooper just nodded as he stood watching.

"I carry these roasted beans with me in these small bags as I travel. One small bag is the perfect portion for a single cup of coffee. I rarely have access to a grinder; therefore, I must be creative when it comes to grinding the beans." He pointed to a long cylindrical item on the counter that resembled a cross between a small rolling pin and a pestle. "A mortar and pestle is my preferred tool, but that is not always available. I can also use this combination roller and pestle and a hard surface. But I have found that this small metal piece can be used to press the bean until it is almost broken enough to brew. Now that you have asked your most pressing questions, what is it that you really want to ask?"

Almost on cue, the water in the kettle began to rumble. As Cooper approached the counter with the kettle that was still rumbling with boiling water, he asked, "Do you want me to pour it over?"

"Patience," Asa replied. "We want to treat our ground coffee with respect. This is part of my process, as well."

Cooper set the kettle on a holder on the counter.

"Have you dried off and warmed up?" Asa asked.

"Yes, still a little damp, but almost dry."

"Well, good then. We have much to do," Asa replied as he reached for the kettle.

Cooper watched as he slowly and methodically poured just a small stream of water over the grounds in each cup. He paused while pouring into one cup and moving to the other. Cooper lost track of how many minutes passed, but it was obvious that Asa was in no hurry to complete the process.

Asa sat the kettle down on the counter. "Now, we wait."

"I've had pour over coffee, but I have never seen this process," Cooper stated almost as if asking "Why do you do it this way?"

"When one travels as much as I do, they must travel light and simplify as much as they can in life. Plus, we often find that more complicated does not always equal better quality. Would you agree?"

Cooper really had no response, so he just slightly nodded his head. He did not want to admit to Asa that he had an incredibly expensive coffee machine in his Houston office, yet somehow he figured that Asa may already know that. He decided to try to change the subject.

"That is an impressive collection of books you have," Cooper pointed to the wall of books.

"Yes, those are what many would consider to be the classics. Are you a reader, Mr. Travis?"

"I read when I was younger. But as I got busy with business and building companies, I read less and less."

"That is unfortunate. Other than a man's spiritual health, there is nothing that feeds the soul more than a habit of reading books that stretch the mind."

Cooper wanted to ask how a man that travels has so many books, but his mind began to wander as he smelled the coffee wafting his direction.

"Perhaps you could begin developing the habit of reading now?" Asa asked.

Cooper paused and thought about how bored he had been. He wanted to say no, but something inside him was nudging him to accept. "Sure, that would be better than just sitting around like I have been doing."

"Then start with this one," Asa reached for a hardbound book on the shelf and handed it to Cooper. "The author was a friend of mine, and the book was written for people like you."

"*The Greatest Salesman in The World*. A book about sales?" Cooper looked up at Asa.

"I thought that would at least get your attention, Mr. Travis. But do not be fooled by the title. The author, Mr. Mandino, experienced life events similar to yours, and I suspect his book will impact you greatly."

Cooper's mind flashed back to the reaction he had when Angel had given him *The Tablet*. He did not want to show the same level of being ungrateful that he had shown Angel.

"Thanks," he muttered half-heartedly.

"Let's enjoy our coffee and get started," Asa must have realized his student was drifting away. Or at least desiring a cup of coffee. He returned to the counter, pulled the bag out of one of the cups, and gave it a little squeeze as it dripped into the mug. He then motioned for Cooper to take that coffee as he finished the process on the other mug. Together, they walked to the rocking chairs and took a seat.

Cooper was excited, but he would be lying if he did not admit to being a little nervous. "What does 'get started' mean?"

"What do you think it means, Mr. Travis?"

Cooper paused and savored a sip of his coffee while staring at the fire. *Should I be cute and smug and guard my thoughts? Or should I just cut to the chase? Probably best to be honest.* "My life is really screwed up. I guess I am to blame for most of the mess. I guess to get started means to find out what I need to do to fix this mess," Cooper confessed.

"True change is a difficult thing. There are usually only two ways that it can occur. One, a person makes a decision that they will put forth the effort to make change in their life and they exert tremendous effort to bring that change to fruition."

"Okay, I think I understand that."

"Two," Asa continued as his peaceful and calm demeanor seemed to disappear with the seriousness of his statement, "A catalytic event or outside force creates so much havoc in one's life, they are forced to act and live differently. In other words, they are forced to change, or they will crumble under the pressure."

"I can relate to number two."

"I am sure that you can. And that is why we are here," Asa's tone went back to the soothing voice.

Cooper saw his opening. "Can I ask a few questions?" Asa sat still and smiled. He may have been preparing to respond, but Cooper did not give him a chance. "Why am I here? How did I get here? And maybe most importantly, who are you?"

"Well, I must say I appreciate your bluntness and honesty. If we are to make any progress, we must be clear as to our purpose," Asa replied. "Let's start with me. My purpose is to connect with people like you and help them on their journey in life. Many would call me a messenger or possibly a sage. Some would say apostle, but that may be a title that is far above my stature. The word counselor could also apply. I guess I would like to think that I coach people like you to help them bring out the greatness that already lives inside."

"You do sound like you could be a sage...or an oracle. In today's business world, you could be a consultant and make a boatload of money," Cooper replied in a slightly snarky tone.

"Money is of no concern to me. I have more than I need, and I truly have more wealth than most people can even imagine."

Cooper's thoughts hung on those words. *Have I ever heard someone speak the way he does? Every single word has depth and meaning beyond his actual words.*

"I think I like the term coach," Cooper's mind quickly flashed back to Coach's funeral and the soccer practice he witnessed a few days earlier. Curiosity made him want to ask if a connection existed between Asa and Coach, but he also knew he needed to stay focused.

"Then you are welcome to refer to me as a coach, Mr. Travis," Asa replied. "Or you are welcome to just call me Asa. As for your questions of why and how, the answer to both is that you are here because you are at a place in your life where you finally desire to identify your true purpose and live the life that you were created to live. You are here to redefine your life. To redefine success. You are here to become the man you were created to be."

He's right. Everything he says is right. But how does he know these things? And how did he know what Angel told me?

"My wife...She said those same words to me about being the man I was created to be. I'm just not sure I fully understand that concept."

"It is my deep conviction that most men live mediocre lives because they live distracted lives," Asa began. "Therefore, during our time together, we will focus almost all our energy and attention on three primary topics. Some would call them principles or laws, but I prefer to use the term *Acts*. We can say with confidence that these are *Acts* that everyone must understand. But very few do."

Cooper cleared his throat.

"Before you interrupt and ask what the *Acts* are..." Asa smiled, "Let me say that we will take them one at a time so that we are not letting our mind wander too far into the future. We shall focus on every minute of every day. Not the past. And not the future. That is another distraction of modern people. They concern themselves too much with either the past or the future without giving all their energy to today."

Cooper made the wise decision to sit and listen while enjoying his coffee.

"Also, there is a purpose in the title *Acts*. It takes effort and requires more than just thinking or feeling an emotion. It is the root of action. These principles are not just sayings or theories for us to meditate on. They are designed to drive everything that we think, say, and do. With an emphasis on doing," Asa paused to take a sip from his mug. "We will discuss each *Act*, but your assignment is to meditate and think about what we are discussing throughout the day. Do not let stray or distracting thoughts enter your mind. In order to make the changes that I know you desire, you must internalize what we discuss so much so that you become what you are learning. This is not a game. This is not anything to be flippant about. This is your life."

Asa paused as he took another sip of his coffee. "I believe you have a notebook or journal that you use to write down items of significance?"

"*The Tablet?* " Cooper replied. "Yes. My wife gave it to me. She said I should be writing down my thoughts during this time of my life. In fact, she even wrote in the inscription the same words you said earlier about my becoming the man I'm meant to be."

"Perfect. I do love that name. *The Tablet* has divine significance. *The Acts* have divine origins also. I recommend you capture your thoughts about our discussions in your journal," Asa stated and then seemed to stare deep into Cooper's soul.

Cooper squirmed a bit in his seat. *The Tablet begins with my attempt to end my life. I bet he knows since he seems to know everything else about me. Wait...* An uneasy feeling crept over Cooper. *The Tablet. Of course. Asa saw The Tablet when I arrived at the villa. Or maybe he saw it on the kitchen table back on South Padre Island.*

With his mind reeling at what Asa may or may not know about his personal life, Cooper glanced over at the man who was shaking his head at his empty coffee cup.

Asa looked back up at Cooper and smiled his warm smile. "I apologize for being so serious. Let's lighten the mood. How is your coffee?"

"I must admit that I am a bit of a coffee snob," Cooper replied. Asa grinned as if he already knew that. "But this coffee is the best I have ever had. What is the secret?"

"It is not wise to give away secrets, but I can tell you that simplicity is the secret to much success in life. I have a special source for my beans, and you have seen my grinding and steeping process. Many times, the best things in our lives are disguised by complexity. Roast the bean, grind it, and add hot water. That, my friend, is all that coffee is." Asa smiled to let that sink in. Then he changed the subject. "Have you met Maria?"

"Yes, we literally bumped into each other once and attempted a conversation. My limited Spanish made it impossible, and I may have said the wrong things. I'm hoping I didn't offend her. That was the only time I saw her. It is almost like she is a ghost or a magician that has the ability to be invisible."

Asa chuckled. "Yes, she has the gift of serving. Which means she can be a servant without anyone recognizing she is serving. Everything at the villa meets your standards?"

"Yes, of course. The food, the accommodations, the staff." *Maybe I should request coffee be added to my daily menu.* He chose not to be greedy, "But I must admit I have been pretty bored over the last few weeks." He held up the book Asa had given him earlier, "I do have a book to read now, so time will pass more quickly."

"Your boredom ends in the morning. Meet me here at sunrise," Asa stated in a matter-of-fact tone, "We will enjoy a cup of coffee, and then our work will begin."

14

Cooper was ready. He could not remember ever being this anxious for something to happen. Maybe it was the boredom of the last few weeks. Or maybe it was because he felt as if he had traveled all this distance just for this day. This training. This meeting. Or maybe something had led him to this place for this moment in time. A little over a month earlier he had felt so hopeless that he was willing to end his life. Today he had hope. Hope that something would change and his life would begin to improve.

Stifling a yawn after tossing and turning most of the night, Cooper walked to the veranda and sat down to wait for smoke to rise from the cottage chimney. The sun was not up yet, but the early dawn light allowed him to see the dim outline of the cottage roof. The smoke would be his clue that it was time to go.

His mind wandered as he stared down the hill toward the back of the property. He had a pen in his hand with *The Tablet* open in front of him on the table. A dim light from inside the house shone just enough for him to write.

The Tablet – October – 5 days later

Today I have hope. I do not know what the day will hold for me, but I am excited that I have hope.

I want to change. I need to change. I must change.

I will focus on today. I will try not to worry about my past and I will not be concerned about my future.

I am focused on today.

Today I have hope.

Cooper looked up from the journal and squinted to see if there was smoke in the distance. A small puff came from the cottage chimney. Without thinking, he jumped up and almost flipped the table over in his excitement. He snatched up *The Tablet* and the pen ready to roll off the edge of the table and sprinted down the path to the cottage.

He wisely paused and took a deep breath at the door. He would have busted through had he not shown some restraint.

"Mr. Travis, come in," Asa's calm voice greeted him as the door swung open before he even knocked.

Once again, the soft glow from the fire and candles had a calming effect on Cooper. He sensed his heart rate dropping considerably as he walked from the door to the fireplace.

For some reason, he was moved to not speak until spoken to when he was with Asa. It may have been out of respect since he seemed to be an elder. Or maybe it was because he felt as if everything Asa said was so important that he did not want to interfere or steer the conversation in any way. Most likely it was because he strongly believed that this man had a secret to share with him and he wanted to submit himself to whatever Asa had planned. Cooper had lived his life always being the planner. He was the leader. The one that was considered the "take charge" person. In most situations, that meant he was always responsible for the results. But that needed to change. His self-made attitude had failed him. He knew the mess that he had created. It was time to let someone else give the instructions.

"You know how this works by now," Asa nodded toward the pot in the fire.

Cooper heard the kettle begin to boil and, without thinking to use the mitt, reached for the metal arm.

"Jesus Christ," Cooper screamed as his hand touched the hot metal. He bounced around the cottage on his toes for a few seconds, almost crying in pain. Fortunately, the kettle remained on the hook and did not crash to the floor.

"My guess is that you will not make that mistake again," Asa said as he tossed a small towel toward Cooper. "The human mind has a tendency to remember when painful events occur. They will then do everything they can to not make the same mistake again. Though not always pleasant, pain is a great learning mechanism."

What? How odd. He's so sensitive and calm, yet just showed me zero compassion.

Using the towel this time, Cooper carefully pulled the metal arm away from the fire and then hesitantly reached for the hot kettle to carry it to the counter where Asa was finishing his manual grinding of the coffee beans. He set the kettle down and shook his burned hand as if the action would make it feel better.

"Give me your hand," Asa commanded.

Cooper slowly moved his red hand toward Asa, who reached out to touch it. Cooper instinctively jerked his hand back as he looked up.

"It will be fine," Asa wrapped both his hands around Cooper's burned hand. He bowed his head, but Cooper was not sure if he was bowing in prayer or just looking at their hands clasped together.

Cooper felt a coolness flow from Asa's hands into the fingers and palm of his injured hand. It was almost like the sensation of slowly sticking your hand in a bucket of ice water. The sensation went all the way up to Cooper's elbow.

"It is better now," Asa said in a matter of fact tone as he let go. He reached for the kettle to pour the water in the cups.

Cooper held both hands in front of his face palms up and marveled at how they both looked the same. It was as if he had never touched the hot metal.

"What just happ—"

"Let's not get distracted, Mr. Travis," Asa interrupted before Cooper could get his words out. "We have much to do."

Cooper looked at his hands again and then back up at Asa and just stared at him while he slowly poured the hot water into the mugs. *Who was this man?*

"Please, Mr. Travis, go have a seat. I will bring you your coffee in just a moment. I have a small card for you on the table. Take a moment to read it while our coffee is brewing. The card explains our first *Act*."

Cooper reached down to pick up the small card on the table. As he did, he noticed his hand again with no burns or pain. Still unsure of what exactly had happened, he turned his attention to the card. It was slightly bigger than a business card, and it was almost square. The paper was a very heavy stock. The handwriting was tiny, but identical to the writing on the envelope he had found inside *The Tablet* before he had left South Padre Island.

Act of Love

Love is unearned, unconditional compassion and understanding for all people. It is not just a feeling or emotion. It is patient, kind, and honoring to others. Love is an action. It is something that one does. We are commanded to Love God and Love others as we Love ourselves.

I will show Love.

I will seek opportunities to honor those around me.

I have not earned the Love that is shown to me. Therefore, I will not expect others to earn Love from me.

I will not judge.

I will be quick to forgive.

I will be a person of compassion and understanding.

My thoughts, words, and actions will be evidence of the Love that flows through me at all times.

I will show Love.

He read it multiple times while his eyes jumped from the card to the fire to Asa and back to the card. Cooper thought about the word on the card and wondered if he was missing something.

This was the secret of his success?

"It seems so simple," Asa stated as he handed Cooper his coffee, "but this is the foundation that most people never gain a true understanding of. Before you even ask, let me say that the word love has been abused and misused so much by society that it makes it almost impossible to have a discussion about this Act. But make no mistake, the basis for everything that our society and culture was created for rests on this Act. It is an Act that permeates every fiber of how we were created and what we are designed to accomplish."

I'm definitely cynical about love. I better choose my words carefully because I'm not sure it even exists anymore in our broken-down world.

"How exactly do I learn this Act?" Cooper asked. "I don't think I understand what it looks like."

"Well first, let me give you instructions," Asa said. "I advise that you carry this card with you at all times while we are learning this Act over the next few weeks. You will notice it includes a definition as well as a confession. Read it silently. Read it out loud when you are able. Meditate on the topic. Write it in your journal over and over." Asa paused as if to let his words sink in.

"What do you mean by confession?" Cooper asked.

"That is a great question, Mr. Travis. Our words have power. They can bring life, and they can also bring death. Therefore, we must be mindful of what we say. Our confession is not only what we say, but it is an indicator of what is in our heart and our mind. Do you understand the power of what proceeds from your mouth?"

Cooper hesitated before moving his head up and down in agreement.

Asa continued, "For us to make significant, life-altering changes in our lives, we must examine our thoughts, words, and actions. We will use these words to program your mind in the proper way. In the way that you were created. You will use these words, these confessions, to program your soul for true success. Is that something that you can do, Mr. Travis?"

"It seems odd to repeat words and read out loud, but I will do my best to develop the habit."

"Excellent. I have confidence that you will be transformed in a short period of time and that will encourage you to make this a lifelong practice," Asa took a quick sip of coffee, "Also, watch for examples of the Act of Love as you are living your life over the next few weeks and as we are doing the work that we will start today."

"Work?" Cooper raised an eyebrow at this new development.

"Yes, work. A friend across the river is a steward for a coffee plantation. It is harvest season, and the rains have slowed down their harvest. He can use our assistance in harvesting the cherry beans before they get too ripe. It will be an opportunity for us to show our love for others by assisting in this time of need. You are fine with putting in a few weeks of labor, Mr. Travis?"

"Absolutely," Cooper quickly replied. Memories flashed through his mind of how out of breath and winded he was while attempting to ride the bike a short distance on the road in front of the villa. Hopefully, he wasn't too out of shape to help with the harvest.

"Excellent. We will occupy our bodies while we train and stretch our soul. Let us finish our coffee. Then you can go back to the main house. Maria should have a light breakfast for you. You will find some work clothes in your closet. Wear layers because it will be cool this morning, but it will warm up as the day progresses. Maria will have a bag with some food for you to bring for lunch. Prepare your heart and mind for a long day of work, Mr. Travis," Asa said the last few words in a whisper, as if he wanted to make sure Cooper was listening.

Cooper finished the last of his coffee before looking over at Asa and smiling in agreement at this new development.

"Very good then. We shall meet on the other side of the gate at the back of the property as soon as you eat and change your clothing."

15

Cooper sat at the table eating his breakfast with the card that Asa had given him in front of his plate.

Act of Love

Love is unearned, unconditional compassion and understanding for all people. It is not just a feeling or emotion. It is patient, kind, and honoring to others. Love is an action. It is something that one does. We are commanded to Love God and Love others as we Love ourselves.

I will show Love.

I will seek opportunities to honor those around me.

I have not earned the Love that is shown to me. Therefore, I will not expect others to earn Love from me.

I will not judge.

I will be quick to forgive.

COACH

I will be a person of compassion and understanding.

My thoughts, words, and actions will be evidence of the Love that flows through me at all times.

I will show Love.

Cooper read the card again as he sat and ate the breakfast waiting for him just as Asa had said.

He thought about Angel. He knew that he loved her. But the words "unearned and unconditional" kept rolling around in his mind. He realized he did not display this type of love with his wife. And she had been trying to let him know that for some time now.

He had been raised with a strict set of rules. His father never showed him compassion. In fact, his father would say that compassion was a sign of weakness, and Cooper had adopted the same attitude as he reached adulthood. That attitude was how he had built his business. And now all of that was gone. That was also the same attitude he had in his relationship with Angel. And now that was gone.

As much as his pride hated to admit this, the way he had done things did not really work. It was time to make a change.

Cooper stooped to go through the small gate. As he straightened up, he discovered Asa standing in front of him with a smile on his face and two bicycles by his side. He was wearing the same thing he had worn every time Cooper had seen him—khaki slacks, a long-sleeved shirt, and a jacket that resembled a sports coat.

"How are your bicycle riding skills?" Asa asked with a grin on his face.

"Not as rusty as a few weeks ago. I'll try to keep up," Cooper replied as he looked at the bikes and back at the gate. *How did those bikes make it through that small opening? I can barely fit through there.*

"We will follow this trail down to the river. Then we will cross over the river at the bridge downstream."

"I have been to the bridge," Cooper interrupted.

"Wonderful. On the other side of the bridge, we will follow the trail to a road that will lead us up the hill to Juan's coffee plantation."

Cooper looked at his bike skeptically. *I hope I can make it that far. Just the short distance I rode the other week made it hard enough to catch my breath, and this ride sounds a lot worse.*

Asa sat on his bike and began to glide along the path. Not wanting to be left behind, Cooper hopped on his bike and followed. The trail was smoother then he expected it to be on a bicycle, and he managed to keep up with Asa down to the bridge, where Asa paused as if to allow Cooper to catch his breath.

"It is all uphill from here, Mr. Travis," Asa called out as he started to pedal.

And he was correct.

Not wanting Asa to get too far ahead of him, Cooper's competitiveness kicked in, and he pushed harder and harder. When he finally stopped at the end of the three-mile upward climb, his heart was beating out of his chest and sweat poured down his face.

He spotted Asa, who didn't look winded at all, greeting a group of men gathered on the side of the dirt road. The men, obviously happy to see each other, were hugging and speaking in Spanish.

As he stepped off his bike, Cooper forgot what strenuous exercise does to out-of-shape legs, and he almost fell flat on his face. His legs barely had enough strength left to hold him up. After regaining his footing, he lifted his foot to push the kickstand down. Or at least he tried to lift his foot. It moved but completely missed the kickstand. The bike tipped away from him, and since he had almost no strength left to hold himself up, he fell in slow motion to the ground on top of the bike.

The resulting crash interrupted the party, and much to Cooper's embarrassment, all the men hurried over. He stared at the assortment of shoes, boots, and sandals that filled his vision, and he inwardly groaned. His manual labor experience had gotten off to a crashing start. He was sure the men were impressed with this city boy who had arrived to save the day and help with the harvest, but was now sprawled across his bicycle.

Assuming it would be easier to stand up from a seated position, Cooper rolled onto his back while still lying on the bicycle. Handlebars, pedals, the seat, or something now stuck in his backside. But as much as he tried, his Jell-O legs refused to let him stand up. Finally, three of the men bent down and lifted him off the ground. He wobbled as his legs bore his full weight.

"Mr. Travis, is everything okay?" Asa asked.

"My body is not in great shape, but nothing can compare to the damage my pride is taking right now."

"Pride is a cancer that will eat the strongest person from the inside out. Never let what others think of you control who you are," Asa spoke in a calm voice. "You have come to assist these men during a challenging time, and they are grateful and offer you unconditional love...even if you do have difficulty standing up."

Cooper noticed a slight smile perk up in the corner of Asa's mouth as those last words flowed out. He also noted Asa's use of the phrase "unconditional love."

"Mr. Travis, I would like you to meet Señor Juan Diego. He is the steward of this plantation."

"Buenas dias, Señor Travis," Juan reached out to shake Cooper's hand, but also gave him a strong hug, "We are thankful you here. When coffee cherries get ripe, it takes much work to bring them in."

Cooper realized he knew nothing about what he was about to do. He knew coffee grew on trees, but he had never seen a coffee cherry. Since he was not wanting to cause himself any additional embarrassment, he chose to keep that fact to himself.

"You speak English?" Cooper asked, relieved that he would not have to go through the same awkward exchange he had with Maria.

"Yes, not so good. But okay," Juan replied.

"And do I call you Juan?" Cooper used the usual routine he followed whenever he met a new business contact—greeting, name, and attempting to connect in some way. It had served him well in his old business world, so maybe the same principles would be acceptable here.

"Here in our country, we have mucho names. My family name is Juan Diego Castro Guzman. But you call me Juan."

"Thank you, Juan. It is my pleasure to meet you," Cooper said. His leg muscles quivered a bit, and he feared he would fall flat on his face once again.

Juan turned to his men and spoke at such a speed that Cooper thought he may be mad or upset. When the men walked away, he realized that whatever Juan had said meant that it was time to get started.

Asa, as if he knew that Cooper was struggling to stand, stepped to his side and held him under his left arm.

"Mr. Travis, we will be harvesting ripe coffee cherries over the next few weeks. As you may know, the cherries hold the precious beans that are roasted and loved by many. You have told me you have a deep appreciation for coffee. You will grow to appreciate it even more over the next few hours, days, and weeks."

"I am not sure that I have the skill or the energy to help much," Cooper replied as Asa steered him toward the group gathered next to an old truck by the road.

"It is very hard work, but that may be good medicine for you during this time of your life. The process is simple. You will take these buckets and strap them to your body. We will then walk through the orchard, and you will gather the red coffee cherries only and place them in your bucket. As the buckets fill, we will gather the cherries in large burlap bags and place them on the truck," Asa explained.

Cooper attempted to process his assignment. The buckets were nothing more than modified laundry baskets, and the burlap bags were piled up on the side of the road behind the truck. The other men grabbed their buckets, hung the rope attached to the buckets around their neck, and walked into the grove of trees to Cooper's left.

"Those trees look pretty tall. How do we reach them?"

"The tall trees are not coffee. They are avocados. Coffee does best when it is not in the direct sun all the time. So larger trees like the avocado tree are planted in the same orchard to provide some shade. The coffee is about our height which will make it much easier to collect."

Nothing about this day seemed easy to Cooper. It had started with him burning his hand only to have it miraculously healed. Then he was handed a card that had a definition of love that was nothing like the definition he thought he knew. He had followed an old man down a path in the jungle of Costa Rica on a bicycle ride that almost killed him. And now he was taking a plastic laundry basket into a coffee and avocado orchard to pick coffee cherries all day.

All of this was before eight o'clock in the morning. *What else could this day lead to?*

16

As his head hit the pillow he tried to identify what parts of his body did not ache. None. They all hurt. He barely had the strength to raise his arm to read his small card.

Act of Love

Love is unearned, unconditional compassion and understanding for all people.

He attempted to focus on the words unearned and unconditional, but his mind seemed to drift. Then it drifted off a cliff into nothingness.

A loud banging on his door startled him awake. He sat up quickly in bed and noticed light streaming through the windows. At the same time, the muscles in his back let out a scream. He laid back down, and everything in his body told him not to get up. But he heard Asa's words speaking in his ear, "It will be an opportunity for us to show our love for others by assisting in this time of need."

Love is an act. I will show love.

Cooper stared at the ceiling. *I don't know exactly what that means, but this out-of-shape body of mine is trying to keep me in bed. I can't show love to others if I don't get up.* He used all his energy to swing his legs to the floor and sit up on the edge of the bed. His eyes noticed the card on the floor. He reached down to pick it up, but instead of leaning over, he fell flat on his face. Again. *So much for my legs working today. If they can't hold me up while I'm sitting, what's going to happen when I stand up?*

He struggled to raise himself to a sitting position. As he sat on the cool tile floor, he reached out for the card. He read it silently at first. Then he remembered one of Asa's instructions. He spoke out loud even though it was just a little more than a whisper. He actually felt energy move through his body as he spoke.

> *Act of Love*
>
> *Love is unearned, unconditional compassion and understanding for all people. It is not just a feeling or emotion. It is patient, kind, and honoring to others. Love is an action. It is something that one does. We are commanded to Love God and Love others as we Love ourselves.*
>
> *I will show Love.*
>
> *I will seek opportunities to honor those around me.*
>
> *I have not earned the Love that is shown to me. Therefore, I will not expect others to earn Love from me.*
>
> *I will not judge.*
>
> *I will be quick to forgive.*
>
> *I will be a person of compassion and understanding.*

My thoughts, words, and actions will be evidence of the Love that flows through me at all times.

I will show Love.

He repeated it louder this time, and he felt compelled to get off the floor as he said it. He dressed as quickly as he could and went to the kitchen. He spotted his breakfast tray on the veranda and walked outside. A note rested on the table beside the tray.

My apologies for missing our appointment this morning. I have left to attend the harvest. It will be understandable if your body requires rest. We will meet later today. May your day be peaceful and restful.

Asa

Cooper paused. Rest would be nice. Then he pulled his card out of his shirt pocket and read it to himself.

"As pitiful as I seem now, there are people that need me to show up," he whispered and almost gritted his teeth at the same time.

He finished a few more bites, picked up the small burlap satchel filled with his lunch, and began walking down the hill to the back gate.

Pedaling up the hill, his legs felt like cinder blocks. His body bounced between feelings of extreme muscle fatigue and almost throwing up. Despite the nausea and his heavy, labored breathing, he whispered "I will show love" over and over as he pedaled.

He should have been excited when he saw the truck in the road a few hundred feet ahead, but the sinking realization that this was just the beginning of his day stole his excitement. As he set his bike beside Asa's, Juan came walking out of the orchard toward the truck.

"Pura vida, Mr. Travis, it good to see you. Do you feel ok?"

"A little stiff from our hard work yesterday, but I made it here and will do all that I can to help today."

Juan shook his hand and gave him a strong hug, "We thankful for you to help. You are a man of understanding and compassion. This is important to our families, and you helping means much. It is honor to have you here."

Cooper smiled when Juan used the words *compassion* and *understanding* and *honor* because he was sure that Asa had told Juan what to say. But Juan did not return the smile, and his face failed to acknowledge that he knew why Cooper was smiling.

Cooper decided to leave it at that, and he reached down to collect his modified laundry basket before walking into the orchard to begin his daily harvest.

———

The days at the orchard were long and tough. One would think that monotony would set in after a while, but Cooper found satisfaction in completing the work. It was not mentally tough, but there was a skill involved. He learned that some harvesters of coffee cherries just strip all the cherries—green, orange, ripe red, and overripe brown—from the branch. Juan and his crew took pride in only picking the cherries that were ripe and ready, leaving the unripe ones to harvest later. Every morning, Juan gave instructions on what area the pickers were to concentrate on that day. They would then fan out and cover a portion of the orchard.

Cooper had spent the first three days learning and understanding the process and finding a rhythm. Asa had stayed close to Cooper during that time and followed along whispering instructions and corrections.

"Just relax and let the work come to you. Pick the branches in an up and down pattern as you move down the row," Asa repeated over and over as if picking were a religious experience.

Cooper's mind wandered at times whenever he reached the point that every muscle in his body ached. He laughed out loud occasionally when Asa repeated his "relax and let the work come to you" saying because it reminded him of something from *Caddyshack* or *Karate Kid*.

Asa stared back at Cooper with a blank look as if he had no understanding of the pop culture references.

As Cooper's body became acclimated to the schedule and work, he began to embrace the job and really enjoy it. Plus he was noticing a difference in his physical strength and endurance.

When the pickers brought their full baskets back to the road, the coffee cherries were dumped into the large jute bags. Once the bags were full, they were cinched and closed. A few times during the day, the men lifted the bags and carried them to the nearby truck. Cooper guessed that each bag weighed at least a hundred pounds. Probably more.

On his second day, Cooper had attempted to lift one of the bigger bags. Except he could not even get it to budge off the ground. He felt slightly embarrassed...again...when Asa walked up and suggested they pick up the bag together. Cooper helped a bit, but Asa bore the weight of the bag. Cooper then stepped aside and marveled as Asa picked up the next bag and placed it on his shoulder in one smooth move. Effortless. And then he did it again and again and again.

By the end of the first week, Cooper was able to lift a bag slightly and drag it. After another week, he could lift the bag about waist high, but it was a struggle.

He felt pretty accomplished by the fourth week when he could throw a bag onto his shoulder and push it into the truck.

The days started early when the air was cool. At times, clouds or fog hung over the orchard and plantation. As the sun rose high in the sky in the middle of the day, the air would start to heat up and get warm.

Cooper was amazed at Asa's ability to work all day during the cool and the heat without straining or sweating. Asa never struggled. Or at least he did not let anyone see him struggle. And he stayed dressed in the same attire all day including the jacket that he wore. Cooper noticed that the only time Asa removed his jacket was when they moved the large bags full of cherries to the truck.

As the day heated up, the other men would shed layers of clothing. Cooper sometimes got so hot he stripped off his shirt. Others on the crew did the same, but Cooper was the only one with such a white stomach that he could have been a beacon.

Two weeks after he started working, and around what he assumed was the beginning of November, he noticed that his glaringly white skin had gone from pink to red to golden brown. He also noticed the squishy belly he had started with had disappeared. He had never spent much time in the gym after his high school and college days, so he quickly admitted that he enjoyed seeing what this manual labor did for his physique. Plus, he was probably eating the healthiest diet he had ever eaten in his life.

Every day, Maria prepared breakfast fresh and packed a burlap bag for him to take to the field. His bag typically contained some fruit and a tortilla wrapped around rice, beans, a sauce, and either chicken, beef, or pork. Maria also included some fried plantains. He had grown up as a particular eater, but by the time they took a short break for lunch, he was usually so hungry he could have devoured the burlap bag, if possible.

Juan and a few of the crew sometimes picked the hard, firm, and not yet ripe avocados off the trees as they passed through the orchard. They would place the avocados in the truck, and a few days later they would be ready to eat. Cooper was used to seeing people prepare avocados by cutting and peeling them and removing the pit, but the crew ate them like an apple, skin and all. A few carried salt with them and sprinkled it on the avocado to make it taste even better. At first, Cooper felt funny when he tried eating an avocado that way, but the convenience and the taste grew on him. He ended up eating at least one avocado every afternoon, and it became an enjoyable part of his day.

Maria seemed to know that Asa needed something to eat also, at least on the days that Asa ate. One day each week, Asa skipped lunch. He told Cooper those were days he rested his body by allowing it to skip food. He never used the word *fasting*, but Cooper was smart enough to know that was what he was doing. Cooper's body craved food because of all the energy he was expending, so he had a hard time imagining what would happen if he skipped a meal, much less an entire day of eating.

On the days that Asa chose to fast, he did not sit with the crew during lunch. Instead, he walked off down the dirt road. When Cooper asked what he did while walking alone, Asa replied that solitude and silence are important to gaining clarity in life. Cooper thought back to the weeks he had spent at the villa waiting for Asa to begin working with him. He did not think he had gained clarity during that time. If anything, it had only fueled his anxiety.

Whenever they did eat together, the conversations they had were enjoyable and it always stretched him. Cooper attempted to find out more about Asa's past, where he was from, and what his background was, but Asa's answers were vague. He was never rude when answering, yet somehow he always brought the conversation back to Cooper and what his life was like rather than answer Cooper's questions.

Asa also spent a good bit of time reinforcing the Acts and teaching Cooper.

A few weeks into the harvest, Asa asked Cooper, "Now that you have meditated on the *Act of Love*, tell me, what have you loved during your life?"

Cooper hesitated for a long time. Since they were taking their lunch break, the silence did not seem as uncomfortable as Cooper was while thinking. "I have considered that over the last few days. When you first handed me the card, I will admit that I was a little disappointed. My hope was that you would have some magical formula or wisdom that I could use to snap my fingers and change my life. Love did not seem like the wisdom I was looking for."

"Is that because you have mastered this principle, Mr. Travis, or is it that you have never experienced it?" Asa had a way of asking questions that seemed simple, but they could cut through a man like a knife going through warm butter.

Angel. I know she loves me. And I'm in love with her. But is it really unearned and unconditional compassion and understanding? Do I honor her? Am I forgiving?

Probably not.

"I think if you had asked me that question a few months ago, I would have responded yes out of ignorance and a misunderstanding of what your definition of love really is. But the more I think about it and meditate on what you are teaching, I doubt that I know what love is," Cooper sighed and slumped a little as he sat in the shade on the side of the dirt road.

"It is nothing to be ashamed of, Mr. Travis. You and most of the people in the world have been fooled into thinking that you know what is critical in life. But, in reality, you are chasing after something you will never achieve."

What does that even mean? Before he could ask, Asa continued.

"People in modern society seem to think that success is achieved by acquiring things and friends and spouses and children. And there is nothing wrong with any of those. But without the foundation and understanding of the true meaning of love, none of those will bring joy to someone's life. Do you agree?"

Cooper did not have to think about it. Someone could have looked at him not too long ago and said that he had all those things, but yet he was so distraught that he was willing to take his own life. His life was proof that Asa was correct. He chose to just nod in agreement rather than voice his thoughts.

"Can I ask you a question, Mr. Travis?"

Cooper continued nodding.

"Can you remember when you first met Angelina? Would you tell me that story?"

"Interesting that you called her Angelina. That is her real name, but everyone always calls her Angel. Did I tell you her real name?"

"I just assumed her given name was Angelina," Asa replied.

Cooper paused as his mind drifted back into his memories almost fourteen years to when he had met Angel.

"I was twenty-six. Just finishing up graduate school," Cooper started the story, "And I thought I was a big shot. Graduate school was one of the requirements that my father had placed in his will for me to achieve before I was thirty."

"What were some of the other requirements?" Asa quizzed Cooper.

"Undergraduate degree with good grades. Graduate degree. No legal challenges. He left small amounts of money that I had to invest and report back to the trustee on how I had managed the investments. All of those were pretty easy for me. I wasn't the best student at the University of Texas, but I could get things accomplished when I was forced. The toughest requirement was that I had to be married by the age of thirty."

"Your father's will required you to be married?" Asa raised his eyebrows in obvious surprise.

"Yes, it sounds crazy now. But, at the time, I wasn't concerned," Cooper shrugged his shoulders. "I never had any issues dating or being around women. I just thought I would find someone before the deadline and cash in."

"That does not sound like a good formula for a lifelong relationship, does it, Mr. Travis?"

"It doesn't now. But back then I was not thinking long term. I was just doing all I could to gain my inheritance. And I was pretty cocky about the whole thing. Angel changed some of that."

"Yes, let's get back to how you met," Asa steered the conversation.

"I was getting to that. My buddies and I all thought we were important and that we were being prepared to take over the world. We would go to the bar in the Driskill Hotel in Austin and act like we owned the place. We sipped expensive whiskey and were loud and obnoxious. Angel was a waitress there. She was twenty-one and working her way through school. She worked hard. That is a tough job, and she would work late and then get up early to study and attend class. I had it easy compared to her."

Asa nodded with a slight grin on his face.

"It was difficult for her to walk in a room and not turn heads. Both men and women noticed her beauty. And perhaps she was even more attractive because she acted as if she did not know how good she looked. She had black hair and brown eyes. Her skin had that perpetual tan look. And her teeth were electric white against all those natural shades of brown and black. She was beautiful. She smiled all the time when we first met. The years she spent with me caused her to smile less and less."

"Let's stay focused on how you met," Asa insisted.

"It really was love at first sight for me. Or at least my definition of love. Maybe a little bit of lust at first sight, too. But it was college, and lust controls most men in their early twenties, right?" Cooper lamely attempted to justify his actions.

Asa did not give any indication of agreement.

"I always acted cool, but my whole demeanor changed that night I saw her the first time. When she showed up to take our order, I lunged forward in my seat. All my friends noticed her, too. Everyone sat up straight and stuck out their chest. Yes, her legs were stunning, and her skirt did not hide how nice they looked. But I was mesmerized by her smile and warm brown eyes. Up to that point in my life I think I was going through the motions to satisfy my father. But when I saw her, I made the decision that she was the first thing in my life that I really wanted."

"Are you sure you were not just looking for the wife to meet your marriage requirement?" Asa asked.

"Oh no. Well, at least I don't think so. Something just felt different. I played it cool and was able to get her number even though she really wanted nothing to do with me. Or any of my friends, for that matter. She later said she knew our type. I focused and decided to be on my best behavior as we dated, got engaged, and then married. If I had a superpower, it was the ability to focus on something and get it. That focus may also be my kryptonite," Cooper's voice trailed off.

"It sounds like she made quite an impression on you. When did you get married?"

"We waited a few years. I knew she was the one and she wanted to get married. But we waited until I was twenty-nine, and she was twenty-four," Cooper did some math in his head. "So we dated and were engaged for three or four years first."

"If she made such an impression on you, why would you wait that long? Are you sure the marriage requirement from your father's will did not impact your decision?"

"No!" Cooper's voice rose quickly. Asa was forcing him to think about things he would rather ignore, and he did not like what Asa's questions implied. "No. At least, I don't think so. The will did start causing me to think. And I liked that she didn't care about my money or inheritance. But she was so different from me that it almost scared me."

"In what ways do you refer?" Asa continued to press Cooper.

"I was calm and reserved. She was calm most of the time, but she could flip a switch and get excited and animated. In many ways, that is what I loved the most about her. She had the ability to show emotions in a way that was foreign to me. But it also made me nervous. I think it scared me because I could not control it. Over the years, I gradually made her change. I was good at molding people around me to get to an end result. I also had a need to control everything and everyone. That may even be why I called her 'my Angel' all the time. Not so much a term of affection, but more a term of possession or control."

"Is controlling someone the same as loving someone?"

"No. It is not," Cooper sighed.

"Control is actually giving someone conditions and forcing them to earn your affections. That is not love, Mr. Travis. That is manipulation and very selfish," Asa was direct in his assessment.

"You are correct, and I realize that now."

"Is that need to control in the past? Or do you still have that need and desire?"

"I hope that the desire to control others is part of my past. Not my future."

"Good. Now that you have studied what love means, you really do love her. Is that a correct statement?"

"Yes. Yes, I love her. I love her more than I ever have, and I realize that now," Cooper smiled as he figured out why Asa had wanted to hear their love story. "I just wish I could let her know that so I can make up for all my mistakes."

"Then we are closer to where we need to be. Let's get back to work, shall we?"

17

She stole his heart almost immediately. He was not sure what day she had actually started working in the orchard, but it seemed like she had been by his side the entire time. Dark hair, brown eyes, and a smile that made Cooper feel warm all over. Just like Angel had done.

The harvest had been going well, but Juan wanted to pick up the pace so they could get ahead of schedule. He kept track of where they had already picked the cherries because he knew that in a few weeks they would pick another round in that same location in order to select the cherry beans that had ripened since the first picking. He asked the crew if any of them had friends or family that wanted to help and make some extra money. To set the example as the leader, Juan had his family—his wife, two sons, and a daughter—work a few days per week even though the children would miss school.

One day at lunch, she walked right up to Cooper while he was eating and said, "Hello there. My name is Rosa Angelica. But almost everyone calls me Pooh. Especially my friends. You are welcome to call me Pooh also. I'm eight years old. It is very nice to make your acquaintance."

His jaw may have actually dropped as Cooper stared at the girl speaking with a British accent in Costa Rica. He stood up because he just felt as if that was the proper response.

"Well, it is very nice to meet you, Rosa Angelica. My name is Cooper Travis," He reached his hand out.

"Please, call me Pooh," She firmly shook his hand, "I can sense that we will be great friends."

"Can I ask you a question?"

"Why, of course, you may."

"I am curious about how you have developed the accent you have. It does not really seem to fit this…area."

She put her hand to her mouth to muffle her giggle, "I do understand why you would consider my accent odd. It is actually very simple. When I was a baby, my parents would sit me in front of the television, and I watched Winnie the Pooh videos, and I fell in love with them. I watched them over and over again and again before I even started speaking. My parents were surprised when I began speaking and I sounded just like Christopher Robin."

"Christopher Robin?" Cooper hesitated for a second before figuring out the connection, "Oh, you do sound like Pooh's friend Christopher Robin! I can hear the resemblance now. I watched some of those movies, but obviously not as much as you. I still speak Texas English."

Pooh giggled again and put her hand to her mouth as if to hide the sound.

The work was tough, but Cooper found his daily rhythm by what he assumed was the middle of November. Coffee with Asa in the morning. Riding his bike to the orchard. Greeting Pooh. Retrieving the buckets and assignments from Juan. And walking off into the orchard.

Cooper's heart melted every time Pooh reached up and held his hand as they walked.

"I will pick the low branches. You get the high branches. We can be a team," She would use a tone that was not bossy, but definitely commanded attention.

"That sounds great" was Cooper's usual reply. It was funny how he tried to speak with better diction and enunciation when he spoke to her. He even found himself attempting to mimic the British accent.

Cooper and Asa sometimes talked at lunch, but on the two or three days that Pooh worked in the orchard, Asa and Cooper enjoyed some time together later in the day at the cottage. Asa often asked questions about love, and Cooper's answers led them into a deeper conversation. However, the harvest days were so long that it was all Cooper could do at night after leaving Asa's cottage to get back up to the villa, eat a bite, and then fall into bed.

As much as Cooper enjoyed spending time with Asa, he found himself enjoying his time with Pooh more than anything. She was extremely smart, but her innocence and attitude were infectious. The more time he spent with her, the more his heart ached for a child of his own. Not just a child of his own, but a child with Angel. Picking the coffee cherries allowed him time to think and meditate, and he often thought about how he and Angel had talked about having children, but he always told her the time was not right. Now he realized how unfair he had been in ignoring her desire to have children. He regretted not slowing down and showing her some compassion.

Something was softening inside him, and he was understanding the importance of his first lesson more and more. Every word and line of the *Act* stretched Cooper, but the last two lines were so challenging that he wondered if they were even possible. *My thoughts, words, and actions will be evidence of the love that flows through me at all times. I will show love.*

"Would you be available to join me at my school for lunch on Friday?" Pooh asked during a lunch break early in the week.

Cooper looked up at Asa whose smile encouraged him to agree. *How can I say no to such a simple and sweet invitation?* "I would be honored, but I need to check with my boss to make sure I can have the time off."

"I am sure we can arrange some time off for you," Pooh answered with a smile and a tilt of her head toward her father.

Juan nodded his agreement and insisted that Cooper take the entire day off on Friday. And Asa encouraged Cooper to sleep in and spend some quiet time reflecting on what he was learning.

Since he would miss his coffee time with Asa Friday morning, Cooper asked him if they could sit in front of his fire to relax and talk without feeling rushed the night before.

"How are you doing, Mr. Travis?" Asa asked Cooper as they both sat in the rocking chairs staring at the fire.

Cooper paused before answering. He had his hands wrapped around the coffee mug, and he continued gazing at the flickering flames. The warmth of the fire and the coffee penetrated his soul and softened it,

"I feel different. I am not sure that my circumstances have changed for the better. But there is definitely something going on inside me."

"Tell me more," pressed Asa.

"My relationship status with my wife has not changed. My business and legal issues still exist. I have transitioned from a successful, wealthy business owner to a fugitive working on a coffee plantation in Central America." Cooper paused and let his words hang in the air somewhere between the rocking chairs and the fire. Asa did not interrupt. "I feel as if I should be stressed and possibly even miserable because of what is going on in my life. But for some reason, I feel good. And we have discussed only the *Act of Love*?"

"I enjoy hearing you speak this way. It is a reflection of being authentic and transparent as we have discussed. It encourages me and provides evidence that we are making progress. Allow me to attempt to provide clarity to what you are experiencing."

Since Asa signaled that he was about to share his wisdom, Cooper leaned forward so that he would not miss a word.

"There are many emotions that one can experience. Emotions are part of our soul along with our mind and our will. They are not necessarily bad, but if they remain unchecked, they can control a person's mind and lead to damaging results. Have you known people that are this way?"

Cooper nodded. "Yes, Angel was very emotional at times. I had difficulty understanding it."

"Let's be clear. Showing emotions is not a challenge. Allowing emotions to control one's mind, will, and life is where the danger lies."

"Danger?" Cooper couldn't help but interrupt Asa. He had never considered the fact that emotions could be a danger to a person.

"Yes, danger, Mr. Travis. And let me remind you that not showing emotion does not mean that a person is out of danger. Suppressing feelings and emotion can often be an indicator that a person is controlled by emotion more than the person that sheds tears for any occasion. Men, such as yourself, fall into that trap in today's culture."

Cooper nodded because he knew Asa was describing him.

"The danger lies in allowing the most damaging emotion to penetrate one's soul. Do you know what that is, Mr. Travis?" Asa paused but did not allow Cooper to answer, "Fear. Fear is the most damaging feeling that a person can possess. It is not just a passing thought or feeling. Fear can begin to permeate every fiber of a person's soul and body. It can then begin ruling their spirit and their entire life. I am not just speaking of fear of heights or spiders or snakes. I am speaking of fear of living, fear of death, fear of success, fear of failure, fear of other men, fear of an angry God," Asa paused again to let Cooper think about that last statement, "Do you know what the antidote to fear is, Mr. Travis? Do you know what will drive fear out of every situation? Do you know what will cast out fear from every person?"

Cooper thought he knew the answer, but he hesitated just long enough for Asa to answer his own question.

"Love. Love is the medicine that cures the disease of fear, Mr. Travis. The reason that you are beginning to feel joy inside you is that you are allowing that medicine to fill your soul and you are sharing that medicine with others."

"Had you shared that with me when we started, I would not have understood what you were talking about. But I know you are right," Cooper smiled at Asa, "I know I have not begun to understand everything that I need to make the changes in my life that must be made, but I like the way I feel now, and I am committed to continuing this journey."

"That is good to hear. You have begun laying a solid foundation for future lessons. Now, it is getting late," Asa stood and motioned for Cooper to do the same, "Enjoy your lunch date tomorrow. Time with those we love is precious. We have no guarantee that anyone will live forever on this earth."

After saying good night, Cooper walked slowly up the hill as the clear sky above allowed the moon and stars to light his path.

"Is life this simple?" He whispered as he walked, "You learn about Love. You work hard every day. And you enjoy a day off to spend with a cute young lady."

Cooper paused as he reached the back porch of the villa. He turned to look back down the hill. The light from the night sky made the plantation and the hills in the distance visible. There was a coolness in the night air, but Cooper still felt a warmth inside similar to how he felt minutes earlier while sipping coffee in front of Asa's fire.

As he looked up at the stars, he spoke out loud, "Life is getting so good."

18

It can be difficult for the body and mind to break a habit. Cooper's eyes opened early on Friday morning. He had wanted to sleep in on his day off, but something inside was nudging him to get out of bed.

After getting dressed, he discovered his breakfast tray waiting for him on the veranda. He placed *The Tablet* and his card from Asa on the table next to his tray. He read the card silently as he ate his food. Then he paused his eating and read the card out loud three times with his voice getting louder with each word.

He looked toward Asa's cottage while holding the card in his hand. The energy that he felt after speaking those words created a rush that was far beyond the coffee that he usually craved in the morning.

When he finished eating, he opened *The Tablet* and thumbed through the pages where he had written the *Act of Love* over and over. He stopped when he reached a blank page and picked up his pen.

The Tablet – Mid-November

I will show love.

Do I really know what love is? Speaking these words over and over again is building my confidence. But I do wonder if I truly understand.

I desire to show love. I want to appreciate and honor those around me.

I do admire Juan and those who are harvesting today. I am thankful for a day of rest, but I miss being with them today. I will return tomorrow with increased energy and focus to achieve our goal.

I love Pooh. I am excited that we can spend time together today. I never knew that children could teach adults so much. I enjoy my time with her more than almost anyone I have ever known and that includes all of my business and personal connections.

I do not know if Angel will consider giving me a second chance. But if she does, I am hopeful that we can have children of our own. My heart is beginning to crave being around children more and more.

Asa has taught me so much. I love spending my time with him. He is pressing me to become a better man.

Plus, I do love his coffee.

Cooper put his pen down and just stared off into the distance. The green hills rolled into the horizon. On one of those hills, Asa, Juan, and the team were hard at work.

I miss being there. They need me, and I need them. Is that love?

Cooper wiped the sweat from his palms onto his pant leg as he stood at the school reception desk waiting for Pooh to meet him. He chuckled as he thought of how he had met with some of the most powerful people in the world—politicians, business leaders, and other dignitaries—yet he could not remember being this nervous waiting for those meetings.

Cooper gave a half smile as Pooh bounced into the school office.

"You made it. Are you ready to have fun?" She reached out her hand to his.

"I think so" Cooper winked. "It has been a long time since I was in school. Will there be a test?"

"No. Don't be silly. You are just here as my guest and friend. We will have lunch first, then I will take you to my class."

They walked down the hallway and turned into the cafeteria. Movement and noise filled the room. Children in navy pants and white shirts moved everywhere like ants swarming a scrap of food. From Cooper's perspective, it appeared to be organized chaos.

Cooper managed to not embarrass himself as he went through the line to collect his tray of food. He followed Pooh through the maze of tables before they sat down at a round table where eight sets of eyes stared at him. It was as if they had never seen a white man from Texas. In between the Spanish chatter, Pooh translated the conversations for him. There was no doubt that he was the topic of the discussions. Not knowing what else to do, he just smiled.

Pooh's classroom was not much different than the cafeteria. It just had less noise and movement. While standing in the front of the room next to Pooh, Cooper counted twenty-one students sitting in short desks in rows. The teacher spoke to the class and quieted them before turning to face Cooper.

"Thank you for being here with us today, Mr. Travis. Pooh has told us wonderful things about you. We are all working on our English. Can you please give your speech in your language? Possibly slow so we can try to follow along?"

"Speech? You did not tell me I had to give a speech," Cooper looked down at Pooh and spoke louder than he should have.

"Yes," she replied calmly with her sweetest smile. "All of our guests get to share about their work and what they do. You can do it."

Cooper sighed. He was now being coached and encouraged by an eight-year-old. He faced the crowd and took a deep breath.

"Well, umm," His voice shook as he tried to speak. He stammered through a painful few minutes of talking without breathing. He knew he was off-track when he realized he was attempting to explain solar technology to a group of eight-year-olds. Some students were staring at him, but others were looking out the windows or down at their desk. Cooper even suspected a few had dozed off. He stopped and turned to the teacher who simply smiled and motioned for him to continue.

He looked down at Pooh hoping she would rescue him and tell him he was finished so he could be put out of his misery. Or at least so the class could be spared any more of his horrible speech.

Pooh looked at the class and then back at Cooper. As she reached out her hand to hold his, she said, "You are doing great. Why don't you tell us about when you were growing up and how you went to school?"

Her smile and her hand relaxed him. He took a deep breath, opened his mouth, and started telling stories. He shared whatever came to mind, but his stories about growing up in Texas and attending a Catholic school just like them seemed to be popular. He lost track of time, but when everyone in the class surrounded him after he finished, he assumed he had done well. He said his goodbyes, gave Pooh an extra hug, and walked with the teacher to the door.

"Thank you for sharing, Mr. Travis. It is so great to see how much Pooh loves you and how much you love her. That is so important for her right now."

"Right now?" Cooper questioned her puzzling statement.

"Well, yes. With her sickness and all the challenges she is facing. She is—"

"Sickness?" Cooper couldn't help but interrupt. He had no idea what the teacher was talking about even though he had spent hours and hours in the orchard with Pooh. He needed answers.

"I am so sorry if I have surprised you, Mr. Travis. Since we had informed our class and those at the school, I assumed you would know. We are hopeful they will be able to get her treatments for a recovery, but that is rare in her condition. I think it is her blood."

Cooper just stood in the hallway staring at the teacher as if someone had just punched him in the gut.

"Mr. Travis, I wish I could speak with you more. But I must get back to my class. Thank you again for visiting with us, and thank you for being a friend to Pooh. You have given her some hope. We can all see that."

After she closed the classroom door behind her, Cooper leaned against the wall and raked his fingers through his hair as he attempted to breath. Seconds turned into minutes as he stood staring at the row of lockers on the opposite wall. Then he turned, shuffled down the hall, and left the school.

19

Cooper lost track of time. The sun was setting over the hills, and darkness was creeping across the villa. *The Tablet* and his card from Asa rested on the veranda table. He had planned to journal and meditate on the *Act of Love*, but instead he just sat and stared off into the distance for hours.

Why did Juan or Asa not tell me about Pooh? Should I be mad, upset, sad, hurt? He felt like something had reached inside him and ripped his guts out. This type of emotion is foreign to me. I don't know what to do with it.

The longer he sat, the more anger boiled inside him. He knew he was building up the courage to confront Asa about lying to him. Or at least not being transparent and withholding information.

Then he saw a small stream of smoke starting to stretch from the top of the chimney into the dusky sky. He stood up and breathed in a long deep breath. Until just a few months ago, he had rarely let any emotions show. Now he was prepared to confront Asa and demand an explanation. The slow walk down the hill to the cottage only fueled his anger more.

"Hello, Mr. Travis. Please come in," Asa cheerfully greeted him as he opened the door for Cooper to enter the cottage.

Cooper walked in slowly without saying a word.

"How was your date with a beautiful young lady today?" Asa asked.

"Good," Cooper's tone was short.

"Mr. Travis, your mood seems disturbed. Is there anything I can help you with?"

"Why didn't you tell me?" Cooper snapped.

"Tell you what, Mr. Travis?"

"That she was sick and may be dying?"

"I see. It seems that you are aware of her condition," Asa spoke quietly with a bit of resignation in his voice, "And you are upset that I did not share that with you when you met her?"

Asa's soft tone helped Cooper realize that announcing that someone has an illness may not be an appropriate introduction. "I guess I just wish I had known about it and not had her teacher shock me with the news."

"So, this is more about you than Pooh?" Asa asked.

Cooper had been standing stiffly near the door until Asa's question broke his resolve. He let out a long breath, walked across the room, and sank into a rocking chair. He thought for a moment before speaking. "It may be about me. But I do think it is more about her. This crazy love lesson you have had me focused on for weeks may be affecting me." His words blurted out as he buried his face in his hands.

"Allow me to prepare us some coffee. We will use this time to discuss the progress you have made."

Cooper sat in silence, staring at the fire, as Asa went through his coffee preparation process. The warmth from the flames, the smell of coffee, and the weeks of programming love into his system slowly melted away any anger still brewing inside his soul.

His thoughts turned to Pooh and how tough it must be for her to face whatever she was dealing with. As he thought about her, tears began to puddle in his eyes and slowly trickle down his cheeks.

"Is there anything that I can do for you?" Asa asked as he handed Cooper his cup of coffee.

"Thank you. I don't know. I felt so good last night. Even this morning, I was happy and in the best mood I have been in a long time," Cooper sighed and wiped the tears from his cheeks.

"Do you have the card with the *Act of Love* written on it?" Asa asked.

"No. I left it on the table at the villa. But I think I have repeated it and written it so often I have it memorized."

"That is excellent. Can you speak it for me?"

"Sure, I have already given one speech today. Why not give another?" Cooper took a deep breath and spoke the *Act of Love* verbatim as he stared at the fire.

Cooper let out a deep breath as he finished and turned to look at Asa.

"Very impressive, Mr. Travis," Asa smiled, "I am pleased that you have embraced the *Act of Love*. Since you have committed this to your heart, does this *Act* say anything about only showing love when we are happy or in a good mood?"

Cooper thought for a moment, "No. It does not."

"Do you recall our discussion about fear last night? Is it possible that fear is exerting some control over you?"

"Yes, it is very possible. I have always wanted to be in control of my life. It could be that my biggest fear is losing control," Cooper studied the flames while contemplating this new revelation.

"As much as we would like to control other people and the circumstances around us, that is not something that is within our power. Man can only control his actions and his attitude. Love is something that we give to others regardless of what the circumstances are."

Silence fell over the room as both men sipped their coffee and stared at the fire.

"There is something else that troubles you?" Asa broke the silence.

"Yes. I struggle with the God thing," Cooper blurted out. He immediately regretted his impulsiveness. He preferred to avoid conversations about God.

"The God thing? Tell me more."

"In the *Act of Love*, it says that we are commanded to love God. How do we even know that there is a God? And how can I love a God that lets a little girl like Pooh get sick?"

"I appreciate your honesty and pointed question. We may be getting to the root of our issue. Many people struggle not just with God's nature, but whether He even exists. We will address that at a later time. For now, can I ask you to assume that there is a God. Do you think that he caused Pooh's sickness?"

Cooper struggled to express in words exactly what he felt. "I'm not sure. It just does not seem fair. She is so young, and she has not hurt anyone. I guess He wouldn't make her sick, but at least He could stop it?"

"That is helpful to know what you believe. There are many that operate with the belief system that God is mean and vengeful and doing all he can to destroy his creation. That would be the furthest from actual truth. I know you are not currently a father, Mr. Travis, but can you imagine bringing children into the world and then using your position as their father to make your child's life miserable?"

"That does not make sense. Why would a father do that? But there are many things that do not seem to make sense."

"We will address your ability to understand God soon enough. For now, what have you learned about yourself and love over the last few weeks?"

Cooper sipped his coffee. Part of him wanted to avoid what was really on his mind, but he felt as if a wave of emotion was welling up inside him and about to burst out. He turned to look at Asa and ask the only question that mattered.

"Is she going to die?"

Asa did not respond. He just stared into the burning fire, the reflection of the flames dancing in his eyes.

Fresh tears streamed down Cooper's face. The lack of response from Asa answered his question. How could an innocent child like Pooh be condemned to die? A sob shook his body, and he blubbered and snotted like he never had in his life. His emotional dam broke, and the news of Pooh's fate unlocked emotions that had been buried deep inside for his entire life.

Asa cleared his throat and rested his hand on Cooper's shoulder, "It appears, Mr. Travis, that you may have passed the test for understanding the *Act of Love*. Tomorrow morning, we will begin the next lesson."

20

The coffee, as always, was exceptional. Every time he took a sip, Cooper was reminded how this simple cup of coffee was the best he had ever had. Earlier that morning, he had decided to focus on his next lesson and not let the events of yesterday consume him. A good night of sleep helped him see things in a different way, plus he felt refreshed.

"What kind of coffee did you say this was?" he asked.

"Special," Asa replied.

Cooper shook his head in amazement at how Asa seemed to always speak the minimum amount of words. Never too many and never too few. In a world where everyone wanted to be heard, Asa was content to say very little. Not only did people speak too many words, but most of the nonsense that came out of their mouths would be better left unsaid. Asa, however, measured his words and spoke with wisdom. Cooper tried to learn from him, but old habits are hard to break. He had spent a lifetime debating and discussing insignificant topics and feeding idle gossip. Now, without being connected to news sources and after spending weeks with Asa, he recognized how shallow his conversations had been for years. He also wondered if he ever returned to society what type of response he would get if he went to his favorite coffee shop and ordered "special" coffee. He smiled just thinking about it.

"Have you ever heard of the Gesha coffee?" Asa asked.

Cooper perked up. He may finally be able to show off his coffee expertise to the wise man that had been coaching him. "I have only had it once. It is considered one of the most expensive coffee beans in existence. Originated in Ethiopia, but Panama is where it comes from now," he paused and then straightened up as if a lightbulb went off above his head. "Is this Gesha?"

"No, but what you may not realize is that there is Gesha coffee that is grown in a very small region of Costa Rica. And to be clearer, you have been helping to harvest it."

Cooper froze as he held a sip of coffee in his mouth. He tried to be stoic, but he could not contain his amazement. "You mean—

Asa waved his hand to stop him, "But please know that this bean you are drinking now has a quality that far surpasses even the Gesha. Only a very small number of people have ever tasted what you are drinking, Mr. Travis. In fact, I estimate that less than twenty people have ever tasted this coffee."

"Where—

"Now, let's move on to our next lesson," Asa interrupted and abruptly changed the subject as he pointed to a card on the table.

Cooper briefly held Asa's gaze. *Who is this man?* He then reached for the card written in the same handwriting as before. Cooper read out loud:

Act of Faith

Faith is the unapologetic and unashamed belief that there is a God and that He is our creator. Faith is the confidence that God loves His creation and has a desire for us to thrive, flourish, and find our place in His world. Faith is hope in a better future and assurance that He has the power, wisdom, and the desire to help me follow His plan for my life.

I believe in God.

I am convinced; nothing can alter my conviction and belief in this truth.

I am not searching for answers. I know the answer. The answer is relationship with God.

I do not always understand His plan, but I know He has a plan and I have a role in it.

I place all my trust in Him.

I was created for a purpose. My assignment is to identify and accept that purpose.

I was not created to fail.

I was created to succeed.

I believe in God.

Cooper stared at the card. His shoulders slumped against the chair. "This one may be tough for me."

"And why is that, Mr. Travis?"

"I am just not sure I believe in this religion and church stuff. It seems to be full of weirdos and mean people wanting to kill or harm others all in the name of their god."

"Yes, I suspected this would be difficult after our discussion last night. Now you know why we started with the *Act of Love*. Most that profess to believe in God have no concept of love. Which also means that they have no concept of the nature of God," Asa said with firmness in his voice.

"I don't quite grasp how God's nature could be love. Isn't God mad at us and sending earthquakes and floods and hurricanes to destroy humans because we are so bad?"

"Well, your mind is much sharper than it was last night. The quick answer is no. It is obvious you have much to learn, Mr. Travis. As with the last card, read it multiple times per day. Meditate on what it says. Read out loud as often as you can. Write it down in your journal. Let the truth of the message sink into your soul."

With that statement Asa stood up as if to silently say, "Let's get to work."

From past experience, Cooper knew that when Asa says get to work, he really means to get to work. The next week of work was grueling with very little time for rest. Cooper did take the time to stare at the coffee cherries a little more than he had previously now that he knew that these cherries created some of the rarest and most in-demand coffee beans on the planet.

He saw Pooh only once during the entire week when she visited briefly to say hello. Her smile brightened his day. He wanted to talk to her about what he knew but decided to not say anything. To him, she seemed tired, but when he asked if she was okay, he only got a big smile, a nod, and "Si."

―――

"How much is this coffee worth when you sell it?" Cooper asked Juan as they were taking a break for lunch one day.

Juan's blank stare back at Cooper provided the answer. Cooper scrunched his eyebrows together. He struggled to wrap his mind around the idea that Juan was not selling his harvest for a profit. *How does someone not see the potential for making a good living? These beans are worth a fortune to the right buyer.*

"Mr. Travis, should everything always revolve around profit?" Asa asked.

"No, but it does seem like a big waste that Juan is not making as much money as he can so the profits could help his family."

"You made quite a large sum of money in your business, correct?" Asa asked Cooper with what looked like a sly smile.

Cooper nodded, and he felt as if he were a fish with a hook in his mouth.

"So, tell me, Mr. Travis, what has all that money done for your family?" Asa drove the stake into Cooper's heart.

"Well, we ate well, traveled, and lived in nice homes," Cooper looked down at the ground, "But now I am not even sure I have a wife or a family...or anything,"

"Plus, you have not had children yet, therefore you may not completely understand the significance of a father's love," Asa gently replied as if to comfort Cooper.

"I guess I don't. My father was rarely around before he died. He worked hard and made a bunch of money for us. I knew he loved me. Or at least I thought he did. But he had his own issues to deal with, and I just decided to work my tail off to prove to him I was man enough to succeed. Actually, his will forced me to work hard to earn my inheritance. And I never knew my mother. She died a few days before my first birthday. I remember nannies more than I remember her. Maybe that's my problem. How could God let that happen to me?"

Asa paused and allowed Cooper to have a moment of silence as he stared off into the grove of trees.

"It is time to get back to work. Continue with your current assignment. We will continue this conversation over a coffee this weekend," Asa abruptly stood up and walked into the orchard with his basket.

"Where is Pooh?" Cooper asked Juan toward the end of the following week. He had missed his brown-eyed friend. He even wondered if his productivity had slowed because his little partner was not there to keep him energized.

"She not feeling well. She told me tell you not to worry. She see you soon."

Cooper sighed. An eight-year-old young lady was showing compassion for him by encouraging him not to worry.

The next day, Pooh showed up at the orchard near the end of the lunch break. Cooper jumped up to go see her. He could tell something was not right immediately because she stood still and did not run to meet him as she always did before.

"I knew you were missing me, so I came to visit," Pooh said in a matter-of-fact tone.

"I sure did. Are you okay?"

"Of course, I am okay. Unfortunately, the doctors are not as convinced. They try to tell me that something is wrong with my blood. But I know my blood is just fine," She stood up straight and forced her shoulders back in a confident pose.

"Yes, of course, you are okay," Cooper let out a weak laugh, "You are here."

"Please do not get sentimental and overly sensitive. You are my very good friend...possibly my best. I expect to live a long life. Possibly a hundred years or more. That way we can be friends for a long time," She gave him a quick hug, turned, and headed back the way she came. Before she disappeared around the bend, she turned back around and gave him a small wave.

He tried to hide the tears welling up in his eyes, but he was pretty sure he was not doing a great job. Deep inside he sensed a tidal wave was about to hit, but he didn't know when or why. All he knew was the feeling had something to do with the precocious child who had invaded his heart.

21

Since the harvest had started, Cooper had fallen asleep at night with no challenges, but tonight he laid awake staring at the ceiling. The card from Asa was face down on his chest. He was perplexed by what it said.

Act of Faith

Faith is the unapologetic and unashamed belief that there is a God and that He is our creator. Faith is the confidence that God loves His creation and has a desire for us to thrive, flourish, and find our place in His world. Faith is hope in a better future and assurance that He has the power, wisdom, and the desire to help me follow His plan for my life.

I believe in God.

I am convinced; nothing can alter my conviction and belief in this truth.

I am not searching for answers. I know the answer. The answer is relationship with God.

I do not always understand His plan, but I know He has a plan and I have a role in it.

I place all my trust in Him.

I was created for a purpose. My assignment is to identify and accept that purpose.

I was not created to fail.

I was created to succeed.

I believe in God.

"Is there a God?" Cooper whispered. "If there is a God, why would he let me go through all of the things I have been through?"

God loves me and he wants me to thrive and flourish?

Cooper did not feel like he was thriving. He was basically a fugitive destined for jail if and when he returned to the United States.

He sarcastically said out loud, "If being a fugitive and running from my mess is how YOU define flourishing, then I am not sure I want to participate in what YOU call love."

He closed his eyes, and his mind wandered to his business and legal challenges. Thoughts raced around his mind like a pinball jumping all over a pinball machine. His legal situation seemed insignificant now compared to Pooh's sickness. Or losing his wife. His mind drifted to Angel. *Where are you, my Angel? Do you think about me? How I wish I could talk to you. Do you still love me?*

Tears streamed down his face as he imagined her smiling at him. She had a look that could make him melt. He tried to think of a time when he had told her what she really meant to him. His tears flowed even more when he realized his mind was blank. He wanted to blame his situation on money. But money even seemed insignificant at this point.

He could hear Asa saying, "You have learned the *Act of Love*."

"How does one thrive when they love, but the love is not returned?" Cooper whispered.

He missed Pooh. The crew had been working hard to finish the harvest, and he had not seen her in almost two weeks. He wanted to ask about her, but was not really wanting to know the details of her sickness. He could visualize her smile in his mind. It made him smile through the tears that were now puddling on his pillow behind his ears.

"I am so sorry that we did not have children, my Angel," he whispered through the tears. Years ago, he had convinced Angel that they needed to wait while focusing on building and growing the company. And then later he reluctantly agreed they would "try" to start a family. But it was only talk. He just made promises that he continued to break, and Angel continued waiting patiently for him to say it was time to start a family. As he thought of Pooh, he wished he could embrace Angel and apologize. Apologize for being cold and not nurturing her through the pain of delay. Instead of showing love and compassion for his wife, he had spent more and more time at the office.

Thrive? Flourish? Ignoring my wife and her needs is a far cry from thriving. What kind of man am I?

"God, if you do exist, I need to see more of this so-called thriving and flourishing," Cooper mumbled sternly. "Show me that you love me. Show me that you love Angel. Show me that you love Pooh," His voice trailed off to a whisper. As he sobbed and slowly drifted to sleep.

Cooper never really asked how long the coffee harvest would last, but one did not have to have experience to know that the job was drawing to an end. Even so, he was enjoying it more and more. The work was hard, but his body was now used to the physical labor, and his mind was enjoying not just the work but the fact that he could see tangible results at the end of each row, each hour, each day. Every day he carried baskets and bags full of harvested cherries to the truck to haul back to the barns. This work was much more rewarding than working in an office and rarely seeing the immediate fruits of his labor.

As Asa and Cooper were pedaling their bikes up the hill to the orchard, he spotted the rest of the crew waiting around the truck. He briefly looked up after stopping his bike at the side of the dirt road, and he saw Pooh standing beside the truck with her hand on her hip. He jumped off his bike and ran toward her. She took two steps in his direction before launching herself at him and wrapping both arms around his neck. He spun her around as she clung to him. The hug felt so good to Cooper that he had difficulty remembering a hug that had felt better.

After spinning a few turns, he stopped and let her slide back down to the ground.

"I am glad you made it today. I have been waiting for at least ten minutes," Pooh snapped in her British accent but a smile filled up her entire face.

"I missed you, too," Cooper said softly. "How are you feeling? You look great."

"I do feel fantastic. Have you been praying for me?"

Cooper paused. He was not sure if his demanding conversation with God the night before would actually be considered a prayer, but it seemed God had responded.

"Yes, I have spoken to God about you," he replied.

"Well, it appears that he loves you and listens to you. He wants you and those around you to thrive and flourish."

Cooper paused and cocked his head to the side. He glanced toward the back of the truck and saw Asa speaking with Juan and the others. Questions flooded his mind as he stared down at this girl who seemed to exhibit more wisdom than most adults.

Did Asa tell her about the Acts and give her the cards? How did she hear my conversation with God last night while alone in bed? Wait. Is this conversation the example I asked God to show me as proof that he does exist and loves me?

"I must go now," Pooh said while holding out her hand to Cooper, "Prior engagements you know. But I am sure we will see each other again soon."

He reached down and held her hand while still processing what she had just said. "Yes" was all he could mutter as he stood speechless.

22

I believe in God.

Cooper kept repeating the words over and over just like he had done with the *Act of Love*. He wrote them in *The Tablet* just like before, too. But something was different. Something was missing. *What is going on?* Cooper asked himself every time he dropped a coffee cherry into his basket. *I cannot place my trust in something, or someone, I do not believe in. How did I reach this point?*

He went back over the last few months and relived the series of events that had led him to where he was now—from sitting on the thirty-eighth floor of a corner executive office in Houston to picking coffee beans somewhere on a mountain in Costa Rica. He attempted to piece together all the odd, miraculous steps that led him to this place at this time, but nothing that happened in between made any sense.

"How are you, Mr. Travis?"

Cooper fell backward as he looked up and saw Asa directly in front of him. Asa swiftly reached out and gripped both Cooper's collar and almost full basket. If not for Asa's speed and strength, Cooper would have tumbled over and rolled down the hill with his basket around his neck.

"Well, other than being scared by you sneaking up on me, I think I am fine," Cooper snapped at Asa. "But thanks for saving me coach," he added as he gathered his balance and stood up straight.

"You seem...disoriented, Mr. Travis," Asa hesitated as he spoke.

"Falling down can be disorienting. But that is a result of my mind wandering and possibly getting confused."

"Confused about what?"

"It seems to be confused about almost everything at this point. I wonder if I am even going crazy. Or possibly in a dream. And I am not sure if it is a good dream or a nightmare."

"So, you think something is a nightmare because you do not have all the answers? Or because you are not in control?"

Cooper stood for a moment staring at Asa. He had not mentioned anything about control. But yet, as he stood there, he realized that Asa's words had pierced through all that had been bothering him. A few months ago, he had thought he was in control of his life even as his life was unraveling. Today, he felt as if he had very little control.

"Is it possible, Mr. Travis, that we were not created to control a world that we did not create, but that we should allow the one that did create the world to lead and guide us as we enjoy the time we have on this earth?" Asa waited for a moment, turned, and walked away.

Cooper stared down the aisle of the orchard. His knees felt weak to the point that he could have tumbled backward and rolled down the hill again.

The harvest season was over. Juan said it was one of the best he and his crew had ever had. Cooper felt some satisfaction knowing that he had had a small part in the process. This harvest—he had never done anything like it before. He compared the joy of working with his hands and using almost every muscle in his body to achieve and accomplish a task to sitting in a corporate office having meetings and negotiating deals and pushing paper around all day. As much as he hated to admit it, this life—this simple life—was so much more satisfying.

Early one morning, Juan called the workers together and thanked them. He reiterated that this harvest had been the best ever. He instructed Cooper, Asa, and the others to finish working in one final area of the orchard, and he said that when they finished by midday, it would mark the end of the harvest.

A few hours later, the workers gathered around the truck with their final baskets. Asa was the last one to arrive. Juan walked up to him and hugged him. Then he put his hand on Asa's shoulders and looked directly into his eyes, "This harvest not be a success without you. Thank you, my friend. Please pray for us?"

The men gathered in a loose knit circle as Asa spoke in Spanish. Then he glanced up at Cooper and spoke in English, "Father, we give thanks for this bountiful harvest. You continue to show us what abundance means to you. We work, and you bless us. We acknowledge your hand in all that we have done here. I thank you for these men and their efforts. Bless them and their families. We know that you love us, and we give thanks for your love and grace. Amen."

Cooper was no expert on prayer, but the simplicity of Asa's words stuck in his mind. It was as if Asa were speaking to a friend, someone standing in the circle with the harvesters.

Pop!

A loud noise that sounded like a gunshot went off, and the group cheered and laughed as Juan held up a bottle of champagne with foam shooting out of the top. He took a sip and motioned for everyone to pass the bottle around the circle. The champagne was not even halfway around when loud yelling could be heard in the distance. An uncomfortable silence fell over the group. Cooper strained to hear what was being yelled, and even though he could not understand the Spanish words, it was obvious from the men's reactions that it was not good.

Then a young man frantically yelling rode into view on his bicycle. As he drew closer, Cooper recognized him as Juan's oldest son. The young man threw his bike down, ran into the center of the circle, and looked up at his father.

Juan's whole demeanor changed, and his shoulders dropped. He looked down at his son and then back up at the circle. His eyes met Cooper's.

"Pooh is asleep and will not wake up."

23

The devastating words rocked Cooper to his core. His chest tightened, and an ache started in the pit of his stomach. He did not know what to do. He glanced at Asa as if to say, "Do something."

He noticed Juan looking at Asa with the same desperate plea in his eyes. This was his child. His only daughter.

"All is well," Asa calmly said as he looked at Pooh's brother, her father, and the rest of the men, "It is in times like these that our true faith is revealed."

Something about Asa's words angered Cooper, and he fought the urge to punch Asa between the eyes for his nonchalant attitude and monotone, emotionless voice. But Cooper stood still and listened as he continued.

"Juan, please take your men back to the barns so that they can return home. Mr. Travis and I will follow the path down to town on our bikes. We will meet at your home shortly."

Juan remained where he was, almost like he was paralyzed and unable to move his feet. Cooper watched as Asa moved over to Juan and placed both hands on either side of Juan's neck. Asa lowered his head toward Juan's, and they touched foreheads. The tears came steadily as Asa whispered to him.

Cooper could not hear what Asa was saying, but Juan's tears flowed for a few moments. Then Juan looked up straight into Asa's eyes. His entire demeanor changed, and he wiped his face, stood straight, and wrapped both arms around Asa's waist. The two men embraced in a long hug. When Juan stepped away, he appeared to have a strength he had not shown before.

He nodded to Cooper and Asa before walking off to his truck where the other men were already loaded in the bed on top of the day's harvest. He drove off in the direction of the barns.

"It is time for you to put your lesson to the test, Mr. Travis," Asa said.

Cooper had forgotten about lessons and harvests. Only one thing consumed him—the ache in his heart because his friend Pooh was dying ... or was already dead.

"Lesson?" Cooper questioned Asa.

"*Act of Faith*. Faith is the unapologetic and unashamed belief that there is a God and that He is our creator. Faith is the confidence that God loves His creation and has a desire for us to thrive, flourish, and find our place in His world. Faith is hope in a better future and assurance that He has the power, wisdom, and the desire to help me follow His plan for my life," Asa responded without any pause or hesitation.

This man must be crazy. A lunatic. A young girl is possibly dead and he is talking about a loving God.

"Pardon my disrespect, but it seems that since God is allowing a little girl to die," Cooper's voice rose to a yell, "that blows your theory out of the water, doesn't it?"

Asa looked directly into Cooper's eyes and spoke in the same monotone voice from earlier. "First, Mr. Travis, she is not dead, so I recommend you not continue repeating that lie. Also, one does not have faith if they only believe when they are in control or everything is going perfect by their standards. Faith exists when we are faced with times like these. This may be a test for you."

Cooper clenched both his fists and felt the urge to punch Asa again. But for some reason he could not raise his arms. His seething rage caused him to stare directly into Asa's eyes. Then he noticed that pool of blue that seemed to go on for forever. As he stared, his rage began to diminish, and an odd warmth enveloped his entire body. He was not sure how to describe it, but it seemed as if something or someone was wrapping its arms around every part of his body. Peace and calm overtook Cooper's soul.

"I choose to expect that all will be okay, Mr. Travis. Can you at least meditate on that thought as we travel to assess the situation?" Asa asked. He was not condescending or sarcastic in the way he asked, but rather Cooper felt it was a plea because Asa knew it would help him.

They rode their bikes down the path toward the bridge. Asa stopped at the bridge to walk his bicycle across. He looked directly at Cooper and asked, "Do you believe that God kills people or makes them sick?"

Cooper paused. He wanted to say no, but then maybe this was a trick question. He suddenly wished they were still riding instead of having this awkward conversation. "I am not sure. I would think the answer would be no. But why would a powerful God allow all the death and destruction to occur on this earth?"

"You are quite the contradiction, Mr. Travis," Asa smiled as he responded.

"Contradiction?"

"Yes. Like most people in our world, you act as if God is all powerful and all knowing when things do not go well or as planned. In other words, you look for something or someone to blame when your life and others' lives are not perfect. But then when things are going well in your eyes, you ignore this all-powerful God and assume that you control your universe," Asa paused to let that statement sink in. "The real question is this, Mr. Travis, do you believe that God exists?"

Cooper stared into Asa's eyes.

"Do you believe that God is the creator? Do you believe that God loves his creation and wants it to thrive and succeed? Do you believe that there are opposing forces to what God desires? If God is life, the opposite is death. If God is light, the opposite is darkness. If God wants you to thrive, then the opposing forces would want you to fail. If God is freedom, the opposing force is slavery.

"You owned a company with many employees Mr. Travis, is that correct? Did you want your employees to succeed and prosper and thrive? Did you have some rules and guidelines in place that you felt would help them succeed? Could you control your employees' every thought and action? And were there things that you understood that individual employees may not understand? If mistakes were made, did you do all you could to step in and make the situation better?

"God created all. Enemies and adversaries have attempted to stop God's plan as much as possible. Even when those enemies appear to win a small victory, like the sickness of a young girl, God will still use those events for the good of those that believe in him. Now, let me ask you, Mr. Travis, do you really believe God would kill Rosa Angelica?"

"No," Cooper replied. "But I—"

"Who benefits the most from her not living?"

"The enemies of God."

"I choose to believe that God is doing something miraculous even when his enemy is doing all he can to spread death. And that God will use all things to the benefit of those that love Him because He wants them to thrive. Do you believe that, Mr. Travis?"

"Yes."

"Do you truly believe, Mr. Travis, deep inside your soul?"

Cooper felt his shoulders slump in surrender as if he had been fighting his next statement all his life, "Yes. Yes, I believe. I believe in God"

"Then let me hear you boldly proclaim the *Act of Faith*," Asa demanded.

Cooper recited the words with no emotion while giving Asa nothing more than a blank stare.

Asa took a step forward, and his face was no more than a few inches from Cooper's.

"Mr. Travis, I request that you say that again. But this time say it with the conviction that your life depends on your belief. Or if that is not enough to stir you up, then make that profession as if a young lady's life depends on your faith."

Cooper clenched his jaw as he stared deep into Asa's eyes. "*Act of Faith*. Faith is the unapologetic and unashamed belief that there is a God and that He is our creator. Faith is the confidence that God loves His creation and has a desire for us to thrive, flourish, and find our place in His world. Faith is hope in a better future and assurance that

He has the power, wisdom, and the desire to help me follow His plan for my life. I believe in God. I am convinced, nothing can alter my conviction and belief in this truth. I am not searching for answers. I know the answer. The answer is relationship with God. I do not always understand His plan, but I know He has a plan and I have a role in it. I place all my trust in Him. I was created for a purpose. My assignment is to identify and accept that purpose. I was not created to fail. I was created to succeed. I believe in God."

By the time he finished, he was yelling at the top of his lungs.

Asa smiled and took a step back. "Remember this day. This place. This bridge. Mr. Travis, you have made the most important decision that a person can make. Congratulations."

Cooper nodded and looked over Asa's shoulder at the river flowing down the hill and under the bridge they were standing on. He tried to memorize the flow of the water cascading over the rocks, the beauty of the lush green leaves, and the sound of the birds. He turned around to watch the water continue down the hill before slowly turning back to Asa.

"Do you believe that God has a plan and that we are part of his plan?" Asa asked.

"Yes."

"And do you believe that our Rosa Angelica is part of his plan?"

"Yes."

"Excellent," Asa replied. "Now you are prepared for your final lesson. We will begin later this evening after we visit our friend."

Asa reached into his jacket pocket and then handed Cooper the now familiar sized card.

"We will not take the time to read it now, but you can begin your study later," Asa said while climbing on his bike and pedaling away.

Cooper glanced at the card before sliding it into his pocket.

Act of Peace

He then swung his leg over his bicycle, stood to begin pedaling, and followed Asa down the path away from the bridge towards town.

24

Cooper sighed. Asa was in no hurry as they rode their bikes down the path. In fact, he seemed to be going slower than when they rode uphill to work at the orchard. The slow pace fueled Cooper's anxiety. He needed to see Pooh, but he might not make it in time at this pace.

Pooh is sick and dying. Someone so sweet and innocent.

His mind drifted back to the bridge.

I believe in God.

I believe in God.

I believe in God.

He repeated that sentence over and over with the same cadence as his feet moving with the bicycle pedals.

When they reached the spot where the trail met the road to town, Asa turned right along the main road and picked up speed. Cooper did his best to follow. As they turned to circle the main square,

Cooper noticed Juan's truck entering the square from the other side. Juan passed in front of Asa and sped down a street that led to the residential area.

Asa picked up more speed, but without increasing his effort. He was going faster, but pedaling at the same rate.

Or maybe my mind is playing tricks on me.

While pedaling furiously to keep up with Asa, Cooper realized he was relaxed. And his mind was almost blank. No thoughts of death. No thoughts of Pooh.

Maybe I'm so focused on pedaling that I'm not thinking. Or something is different. Maybe I really have changed. This God thing might be making a difference already.

As they rode up in front of the house, Cooper spotted Juan standing in the doorway hugging his wife who was sobbing uncontrollably. A small group of people stood in the driveway talking in hushed tones.

Asa approached a man standing near the door and spoke softly to him. Cooper watched as they both nodded in agreement. Asa then walked over to Juan and his wife and put his hands on both of their shoulders. The sobbing stopped immediately. The tears still flowed, but everything went quiet at that moment. Asa continued whispering to the couple for a few minutes before turning around to enter the home. He paused, looked back, and motioned for Cooper to join him.

Cooper realized he had not moved since they arrived. He quickly left his spot next to his bike on the gravel driveway and joined Asa.

"Mr. Travis, would you like to go in with me? The medical technicians have been called, so we will only have a few moments."

Without saying a word, he followed Asa inside. They passed through a dimly lit family room to a small, dark room at the back of the house,

Cooper cringed at the pungent aroma that hung in the air. He tried to identify the smell. It reminded him of dirty, damp clothes left in a gym bag for days, but it seemed different than that. *Perhaps this is what death smells like. I hope I am wrong.*

As his eyes adjusted to the dark room, he focused on Pooh lying on the bed with a small blanket covering most of her body. She was still. No movement other than her chest with its small up and down motion. Her dark complexion had lightened, and her lips seemed to have a purple tint although it was difficult to determine the true color in the darkness.

Standing just inside the doorway of the small room, Cooper felt as if he should be fearful. Something was in the room that he could not see. A presence. A dark presence that he could not explain, but it was there. And it was almost as if life itself was being sucked out of the room. He knew Pooh's body was the manifestation of that void. Life was gone from her. She was near death. One did not need medical expertise to know that.

"I thank you, Lord, for your presence and authority here in this place now," Asa said with a firmness as he lifted both hands. He turned to Cooper and motioned for him to close the door.

When Cooper turned, he noticed Juan and the others standing in the main room watching Asa. As he shut the door, a shadow appeared to fall over the outer room, and the lighting in the small room became brighter. Cooper glanced around to see if a light or window had caused the brightness to change. There was no light in the room. And the curtains remained tightly shut.

"Death, leave this room now. Sickness, take your hands off this young girl!" Asa's voice boomed.

The room started swirling, and Cooper pressed himself against the closed door. There was no air flow, but he sensed movement as if something was fighting to stay in the room.

"Now. In Jesus Christ's name. Go!" Asa's voice boomed again.

The atmosphere became eerily still. Nothingness filled the room.

Asa raised his arms to the ceiling again and whispered, "Thank you, Father."

Cooper blinked at the change in the room's brightness. It was as if a light switch had been turned on, but the light was pouring into the room from all angles — from the walls, the ceiling, and the floor.

Asa then knelt beside the bed and touched Pooh's forehead with his right hand and put his left hand on her heart. He slowly leaned down until his face was a few inches from hers. He began whispering and speaking a language Cooper did not understand and, to his knowledge, had never heard. His mind flashed back to a few months before when he had lain in bed burning with a fever and he recalled Asa hovering over him in a similar position.

Cooper's ability to gauge time was totally negated. His feet remained planted to the floor making him unable to move even if he wanted to. He was in uncharted territory now, and he could not take his eyes off Asa and the young girl. It may have been seconds, minutes, or hours before Cooper heard something that startled him from his trance-like focus.

He strained to hear the slight sound that had caught his attention. There it was again. Pooh whimpered. Then she coughed, and Cooper spotted her legs moving under the blanket.

Asa did not budge and continued whispering near her face.

Her coughing grew louder, and she gasped for air. She was back.

"Thank you. It is good to see you," she said with British diction that was just as surprising and amusing as the first time Cooper had heard her speak.

Asa nodded to her as he stood up.

Without Asa blocking his view, Cooper noticed the color rushing back into her cheeks and lips. When she looked at Cooper, her smile brought more light into the room.

"I thought you had left me without saying goodbye. That would not have been polite," Cooper said.

"I did not leave. I think I was just resting," Pooh replied in a soft, weak voice as she glanced toward Asa.

Cooper scrunched his eyebrows together. *What did I just witness? Surely, she was just resting like she said.*

"Yes, I was just resting. I am all healed now. Don't look so sad, silly," She chuckled through a cough as she replied.

―――――

Cooper opened the door, and Asa walked out with Pooh in his arms.

"She is awake," Asa said to the crowd in the main room.

A handful of people gasped and immediately left the house. Whether they left to give the family privacy or out of shock, Cooper did not have time to figure out. Seconds later, Juan wobbled a few times before pitching forward into a small table in front of the sofa. Wails and screams erupted from Juan's wife. The paramedics, who had arrived amidst all the chaos, quickly jumped into action to make sure Juan was okay.

Asa placed Pooh on the sofa next to her mother and covered her with a heavy blanket. Her color was back, and she was definitely breathing, but Cooper could tell she was weak.

"She will need some food now. Nourishment. Comida," Asa looked at an elderly woman who immediately scurried off to the kitchen, "Shall we leave now, Mr. Travis?"

Cooper knew Asa had asked his question without really wanting a response. He nodded toward Pooh, and she nodded back. As Asa made his way toward the door, people seemed to want to ask questions or at least linger around him, but he was moving quickly enough that no one could stop him. Cooper decided to follow Asa's lead and walk quickly before he was asked questions he knew he couldn't answer.

Asa paused in front of the paramedics who, after attending to Juan, had returned to standing just inside the door, "I believe you will find that the young girl is weak but healthy. But please check her thoroughly so that all can be confident that she is healed."

A small crowd had gathered outside the house, but most seemed hesitant or fearful to actually walk inside. The crowd murmured and parted in front of Asa as he strode over to the bicycles.

Before Cooper could grasp everything that had actually happened, he was riding his bike through town and up the path behind Asa.

So many questions were bouncing around in his head.

One thought dominated all the questions.

All I can do is follow.

25

Cooper opened his eyes slowly. A chill filled the air above the covers, so he pulled the blankets tightly around himself. His eyes focused on the ceiling.

Did I really experience what I thought I did yesterday? Or was I dreaming? Did Asa truly heal Pooh?

He remembered the card Asa had handed him on the trail to Pooh's home.

> *Act of Peace*
>
> *Peace exists when Love & Faith dominate one's soul. That allows an individual to abide in a place of rest. Rest occurs when there is no conflict between the spirit, the soul, and the body. Peace is not a place or an event. Nor is it taken or earned. It is received. It is a state of being. Peace is Rest. Rest is Sabbath. Sabbath is Shalom. Shalom is Peace.*
>
> *I am at peace.*

I am anxious for nothing.

I am content with my past and I do not stress about my future.

I enjoy today and live in the moment.

I live a life of Sabbath. Sabbath is not a day or time; it is how I operate. It is the state of allowing my spirit to be in control and forcing my soul and body to obey.

I believe in God and I allow Love to flow through me. Therefore, I am at Rest.

My life is a life of Sabbath. I live a life of Shalom.

I am at Peace.

Not in a hurry to get up, Cooper contemplated the final sentence. *Am I at peace? What happens next?* The coffee cherries had been harvested. Asa had revealed the third and final lesson. And he had absolutely nothing to do today. Or at least nothing that he was aware of. Nothing on his schedule. No one telling him what to do.

Is my time here finished? Maybe I'll head back to the States soon. Or I could stay here. That would be nice, but it is not the same as home. For some reason, those thoughts did not seem to cause any anxiety. Six months ago, he would have considered his time in Costa Rica a horrible experience. He had spent the last few months in a country that spoke a language that he did not understand, and he had been around people who had no consideration for his company, his titles, positions, or money. He had even worked manual labor in the fields. In hindsight, prison might be easy compared to what he had just been through.

Cooper pondered what other paradigms in life may have limited him or hindered him from achieving or accomplishing things. He thought of his finances, his company, his future...his wife.

Angel. He wanted to grieve losing her. He wanted to blame himself for a failed marriage. He wanted to feel guilty for so many things. But something inside him seemed to warm him. Perhaps everything would be okay. He had hope. Even amidst all his troubles, hope had taken root and was growing inside him.

Cooper read the card out loud again before getting out of bed.

As soon as Cooper's feet hit the ground, he felt the chill from the tile floor. He was in no rush, but he dressed and walked toward the veranda for breakfast. His body felt more rested than he could ever remember.

Just as he had experienced almost every morning for the last few months, a stunning breakfast magically appeared at the exact time that he felt the slightest tinge of hunger. Cooper stared at his plate a moment before eating. He felt the urge to look up from his plate and meal.

"Thank you," he whispered as he looked beyond the western horizon and off into the distance.

Before looking back down at his plate, he caught a glimpse of a puff of smoke coming from the cottage. Asa was up. Cooper really wanted to speak to him to debrief all that had occurred over the last twenty-four hours, but he forced himself to pause and eat slowly in order to enjoy what was in front of him.

―――

"It is good to see you this morning, Mr. Travis," Asa said as he pointed to the rocking chair, "Your coffee is almost ready. I was expecting you to visit."

The smell was intoxicating. Wood burning. Fresh coffee. The fire in the fireplace pushed the slight chill out of the air, and Cooper just took some deep breaths and relaxed.

He paused to take a long slow inhale of the coffee after Asa handed him his mug.

"If there is coffee in heaven, then it would be amazing if it were any better than this," Cooper joked as he took another long inhale before sipping the brew.

"There is and it is. You may be in heaven now," Asa answered in a matter-of-fact tone.

Cooper wondered if he should follow up on that statement. But he simply decided to accept it and move on.

"Did you sleep well?" Cooper prodded. He was hoping to gather more information about yesterday without point blank asking about healing someone.

"I usually sleep well, Mr. Travis. Thank you for asking," Asa replied as he sat in his rocking chair with his coffee. "That is one of the benefits of the last lesson I gave you. When one is at peace, they are also at rest. And when you are at rest, sleep is peaceful and refreshing."

"I have read the *Act of Peace* a few times this morning. Just as Love and Faith stretched me, this one will also be a challenge."

"You were considered successful in the business world, were you not, Mr. Travis?"

Cooper shrugged, "Some would say I was."

"Were you able to relax and enjoy peaceful sleep?"

Cooper thought and then shook his head in disagreement, "Not really. There was always something that kept me up late at night. Or woke me up early in the morning. Or the worst one was waking up in the middle of the night and tossing and turning while not being able to go back to sleep. My mind raced about a million things. And, in looking back now, those things were nothing I had control over."

"Be anxious for nothing," Asa spoke softly as he nodded.

"What?" Cooper asked.

"Be anxious for nothing. Relax. Be at peace. Know that all things will work out for your good, Mr. Travis. Do you know what that means?"

"I did not know before, but I think I know now. Or at least I hope I know. Because I believe that is part of the test I am hoping to pass by spending time with you. Remind me what it means."

"It means that all things will work out for your good," Asa replied with an emphasis on the word "all." He smiled like the Cheshire Cat after repeating his statement.

"I believe that I get it."

"Good, because love, faith, and peace are foundational principles we must embrace. And I perceive that you have increased your capacity in those areas during our time together."

"Thanks to you. I still have many questions," Cooper replied.

"I am sure you do. And we want to address some of those questions because our time together is getting short. But first, we have a social engagement to attend. Juan and his family have invited us to celebrate the holiday at their home later today."

"Holiday?" Cooper quickly tried to figure out which holiday it was, but his mind was blank.

"Yes. Please do not tell me you have been working in the fields so diligently that you failed to remember that today is when the world celebrates the birth of the one that brought peace to earth. The one that reconnected us to our heavenly Father."

Today is Christmas?

He had been disconnected from the modern world and was not even aware of the exact date. In his mind, he counted back trying to remember how long he had been in the country.

The last day that he really had noticed was when he left his office after hearing that Coach had died. The same day he held a .44 magnum to his neck and tried to end his life. Not just once, but twice. That was August 24.

Four months. So much has changed in that time.

Ever since Asa had recruited him to help with the harvest, he had not had much down time. Now, he was alone in the house and decided to sit and meditate on the last few months. Asa had told him he had some errands to run and that they would meet at the cottage later that day before going to Juan's house.

Love...Faith...Peace.

He studied the cards that Asa had given him. He even read the lessons out loud as Asa had instructed. Then he thumbed through *The Tablet* scanning his notes. He stopped when he saw what he had written on the third page.

Four words. Four simple words that changed everything.

He turned to a blank page and wrote:

The Tablet – December 25

I am not sure if I totally understand the Acts, the concepts, these principles, these Laws, these words. But I do know that I am a different person than I was a few months ago.

There are so many things that I do not know. That I do not understand. And that seems odd to say because until recently I would have said that I know everything. How arrogant of me.

I do not understand how the last few months have occurred.

Has my journey been circumstance?

Has it been an accident?

Or has it been part of an orchestrated plan that involved many people?

On the outside, it does not seem that much has changed. But on the inside, everything has changed.

I do not wish my journey on anyone, but I am so thankful that I have been through the storms. I am hopeful that I am now equipped to live in a different way even if I am surrounded by storms.

I will show Love.

I believe in God.

I am at Peace.

Love, Faith, Peace

Three simple words. But simple words that mean so much.

Cooper closed *The Tablet* and stood up. He slowly walked around the villa. No television, no radio. In fact, there were very few electronics in the home. He wondered if that was by design.

He decided that this would be a great opportunity to practice resting and take a nap.

As Cooper's head hit his pillow, he had never felt as rested and at peace as he did in that moment. The long curtains covering the door to the veranda swayed gently in the breeze as he drifted off to sleep.

It was a strong breeze that woke him up. It was not a gust, but enough to get his attention. He was not sure how long he had napped. Four months without a calendar, a clock, or deadlines had shifted his mindset about time. He just assumed that he should not be concerned about being late or early.

After changing clothes, Cooper stood in front of the mirror in the bathroom. He held the card in his hand and read out loud.

> *Act of Peace*
>
> *Peace exists when Love & Faith dominate one's soul. That allows an individual to abide in a place of rest. Rest occurs when there is no conflict between the spirit, the soul, and the body. Peace is not a place or an event. Nor is it taken or earned. It is received. It is a state of being. Peace is Rest. Rest is Sabbath. Sabbath is Shalom. Shalom is Peace.*
>
> *I am at peace.*
>
> *I am anxious for nothing.*
>
> *I am content with my past and I do not stress about my future.*
>
> *I enjoy today and live in the moment.*
>
> *I live a life of Sabbath. Sabbath is not a day or time; it is how I operate. It is the state of allowing my spirit to be in control and forcing my soul and body to obey.*
>
> *I believe in God and I allow Love to flow through me. Therefore, I am at Rest.*
>
> *My life is a life of Sabbath. I live a life of Shalom.*
>
> *I am at Peace.*

He took a deep breath and studied the face looking back at him.

Who is this guy in the mirror? I look so different than when I first arrived here.

He was amazed at what he saw. He looked taller. He was tan. His soft belly had firmed up. His hair was long and wavy with strands of gray scattered through it. He could not remember ever being this lean. His arms and chest were not bulging, but it was obvious that working outside, riding bikes, lifting hundred-pound bags, and eating healthy had impacted his body.

"I wish Angel could see me now."

He knew he looked different physically, but he also knew that was not where the transformation had occurred. His soul had been transformed, almost to the point that he had trouble remembering what his thought process was like before his journey.

Cooper smiled at himself in the mirror.

"Merry Christmas."

26

"If it is okay with you, Mr. Travis, we can chat along the way. We have one stop to make before our dinner appointment," Asa said as they walked at a slow and steady pace after passing through the gate at the back of the property.

"I guess that we are not in a rush today?" Cooper asked.

"We have the luxury of freedom."

Cooper once again marveled at how Asa spoke.

"Have you recovered from your work as a harvester?" Asa asked as they passed the bridge and continued toward town.

"I never thought I would survive the first few days," Cooper laughed, "but it may have been some of the most satisfying work I have ever done."

"The fact that challenges in life can be difficult at first, but over time they become a blessing, is truly a gift. Perhaps that is a foreshadowing of things to come for you, Mr. Travis?"

Asa had a unique way of guiding the conversation. Cooper wanted to ask about Pooh and all that had happened in the last few days, but it was obvious Asa had other topics in mind. "I do not think I would have understood what you just said a few months ago. And I definitely would not have agreed with it. I am still learning, but I do think it is becoming clearer to me."

"You have grown and increased in wisdom tremendously during your stay here, Mr. Travis. I do believe that you are prepared for your next assignment in life."

"It is difficult to accept that I may have failed in my life up to this point. I do believe that I am equipped to succeed in the near future."

"Perhaps the definition of success should be examined more thoroughly. It may be that you and society have been so disconnected from God's definition of success that it makes it difficult for us to know if we are thriving or not."

Asa had made a statement, but Cooper heard the inflection in his voice that seemed to challenge him to respond as if it were a question. "From all that I have heard, seen, and experienced recently, I would say that I agree with you."

"Something still bothers you, Mr. Travis?"

"There are many things I regret and wish I could do over, but only one thing seems the most important. I do wish that I could restore my relationship with Angel."

They walked in silence for a few minutes before Asa spoke, "Hope is a powerful force, Mr. Travis. Often we do not even know that we have it, but we are very aware when we have lost it. Do not lose the hope you have in your relationship. I am confident you will have the opportunity to show your wife how you have changed."

"I do hope so. I will try to keep that hope," Cooper replied softly.

"We are approaching our first stop," Asa announced as they entered the main square of the town.

The building in the square was not large, but it was obvious that it was the focal point of the town. And the crosses on top of the building told Cooper that it was a church.

"So, are we attending a mass or some service at the church?" Cooper asked with no excitement in his voice.

"You seem disappointed, Mr. Travis. No, we are going to support Juan and some of the leaders of the community. They show gratitude to those less fortunate on this special day by sharing gifts and food."

"I apologize if my tone was not appropriate. I am just not a fan of church. I guess if I believe in God now, I must get used to going to church every week?" Cooper carefully posed his question, not wanting to offend his teacher and mentor.

"I agree with you, Mr. Travis. I rarely attend formal church services myself. There is a difference between the church that we see in scripture and the buildings around the world that have the name 'church' written on their sign. Always remember that a personal relationship with your loving creator is more important than diligent participation in the requirements that man has invented in a vain attempt to please God, or worse, to please other men."

Cooper raised his eyebrows in surprise. That was not exactly what he had expected Asa to say.

"Let's show people how much we love them. Shall we?" Asa said as he held open the door at the back of the building.

The crowded room was buzzing, and people mingled in front of tables set up all around the perimeter of the large room. After Cooper and Asa walked in, the sound began to soften, and the room became almost completely still and quiet.

Cooper noticed it. If Asa noticed it, he was ignoring it. Every person in the room stared at them. Or, to be more accurate, they stared at Asa. It must not be every day that a young girl that is near death becomes miraculously healthy in this town. News had traveled fast.

Asa walked partially into the room without acknowledging any of the stares. He looked around before waving at Juan and turning to Cooper.

"Let's visit with Juan. My guess is that he has a gift for you. Later we will go to his home and partake in a celebration," Asa said before walking toward Juan's table as every eye stayed glued to him.

Juan's bear hug felt good. Cooper was not used to hugs, but there was something endearing about Juan's show of affection. The bandage on his forehead was a reminder of his fall during yesterday's events, but other than that, he was as healthy as ever.

"How is Pooh today?" Cooper asked.

"She is all healed and is pleased to see you later," Juan replied.

His section of the event was one of the most popular. Cooper assumed the town wanted to know more about what had happened yesterday, but people seemed genuinely interested in what Juan was giving away at his booth.

Coffee.

Cooper raised the cup to his nose and then his lips. Asa and Juan stared intently at him as he took his first sip.

"This is excellent!" Cooper exclaimed.

Asa and Juan smiled at each other.

"Señor Travis, this is coffee you pick," Juan grinned as he spoke, "This is first from this harvest."

Pride can be overwhelming at times. It is a very strong emotion that can be either a strength or a weakness. Cooper stared at the cup again as he inhaled deeply and then took another sip. The pride that he felt in himself and Juan's crew that had participated in the process of bringing this coffee to his cup was unlike any sense of accomplishment he had ever felt in his life.

"You seem to be enjoying your coffee, Mr. Travis?" Asa asked as they sat at one of the round tables in the center of the church hall.

"Yes, I will not say that it is as good as your brew. But it would be a very close second place if I were forced to rank them," Cooper stared down at the cup while swirling the coffee around. Asa nodded and smiled. Cooper knew he was waiting for him to continue. "I have worked and built companies and made money for most of my adult life. This is a different sense of accomplishment that I have never experienced. The accomplishment is not that I did it all myself. But that I was part of something bigger that created something. That is new to me. The effort was hard work, but it was not a burden. I was sore and in pain at times, but I am very satisfied. And now to enjoy the fruit of that in this cup. I just feel good all over," Cooper said with a smile on his face.

"Would it be permissible to say that you are at peace, Mr. Travis?" Asa grinned back at him.

Cooper paused and considered the question, "Yes, I feel at peace. Circumstances have not changed in my life, but all of that seems okay."

"That is being at rest or peace, Mr. Travis. And it is what the Hebrew word *Shalom* means. Peace, harmony, wholeness, completeness, prosperity, welfare, and tranquility all wrapped up in one word. The Hebrew language can be very complex...one word can mean many things. They can also use the word as a hello or goodbye," Asa explained.

Cooper thought about the *Act of Peace: Peace is not a place or an event. Nor is it taken or earned. It is received. It is a state of being. Peace is Rest. Rest is Sabbath. Sabbath is Shalom. Shalom is Peace.*

"How does Sunday or Sabbath tie in with this concept?" He finally had his opportunity to clarify what that part of the *Act* meant.

"Many people consider the Sabbath a day of the week. And religious people argue whether it is Saturday or Sunday. It can be a day of the week, but it means so much more than that. The best way I can describe it is your state right now. Your spirit, soul, and body are in harmony. You are at peace...rest. That is the true meaning of Shalom, and that is when you are in a state of Sabbath," Asa stated.

"You do not seem to like religion or religious people?" Cooper asked while looking around the church building they were in.

"Religion is an invention of man. It is an invention that is used to control and manipulate, and it may be the biggest barrier to a person having a true relationship with a loving God. Remember, you are never required to go through a man to get to God. He wants a relationship with you, not an organization."

Cooper was surprised at the tone in Asa's voice.

"But please remember Mr. Travis, we are to love all people-"

"Pura vida," Juan interrupted as he sat down next to Cooper and Asa at the round table, "Or I say, Feliz Navidad!"

Cooper wanted to ask Asa some follow-up questions, but Juan triggered a different question, "Pura vida? I have heard that term a few times. What does it mean?"

"The Pure Life. Our custom is to use as we greet and sometimes say goodbye," Juan explained.

Cooper turned his head to his right where Asa was sitting. As Cooper suspected, Asa had something to add.

"Pura vida. Pure Life. Peace. Rest. Shalom. It is what everyone desires even if they do not realize it. Our souls crave it. We were created so that we can live as if every day is Sabbath. Do you understand, Mr. Travis?"

"I do now, Asa. I do now," Cooper replied in a relaxed, but confident tone.

27

The rest of the evening at Juan's home was perfect. They ate. They laughed. They celebrated. They sang. And then they ate some more.

Juan's entire family embraced Cooper. But, of course, he and Pooh were inseparable the entire evening. She snuggled up to his side and laid her head on his arm as the family relaxed while waiting for dessert.

"We have gift for you, Señor Travis," Juan said as everyone was settling in on the sofa and chairs. He handed Cooper a small burlap bag.

"I am so grateful for everything you have given me. This evening has been such a special night. I have nothing to give you—"

Juan cut Cooper off before he could finish, "Please, Señor Travis. It has been pleasure to host you. And please accept. You helped harvest this."

Cooper stared at the solid brown burlap bag in his hands. He was holding five-pounds of the Gesha beans he had helped harvest.

"Thank you. I appreciate this gift and that you invited me into your home," Cooper made eye contact with everyone as he looked around the room.

"Dulce de leche!" one of Juan's sons yelled. And the other son shouted the same thing in unison with him a few more times.

Pooh's British accent piped in, "It is our holiday tradition. Dulce de leche for dessert. I am sure you will enjoy it."

Her big brown eyes stared up at Cooper. She then tucked her head back to the side of his arm.

Juan's wife only spoke Spanish and had said very little to Cooper the entire evening. She handed Cooper his dessert and just nodded. Juan brought out a small tray of coffees for the adults, and everyone enjoyed the sweet treat.

"Do you sell any of your coffee beans, if I may ask?" Cooper asked Juan.

Juan paused and glanced over at Asa.

"Most of the beans are given to the church and other local organizations that feed the hungry," Asa chimed in, "He sells very little of these beans, Mr. Travis."

The room went quiet. Everyone stared at Cooper as if he should be the next to say something. He just took a deep breath and smelled the coffee in his small cup.

"Perhaps you could help Papa sell his coffee?" Pooh looked up again with those eyes that would not allow Cooper to say no.

"Perhaps," Cooper replied, "but let's not let a business discussion interrupt our holiday."

Cooper wanted to enjoy this moment and not let his business mind take over. He soaked in everything as the laughter and conversation continued. Pooh dozed off on his arm. Asa, Juan, and his wife engaged in an animated conversation in Spanish while the two boys played a game on the floor.

Nothing on the outside had changed in Cooper's life. Lawsuits and legal issues were still there. And Angel was gone. But somehow everything had changed on the inside. In his soul. This was peace, rest, shalom. Cooper was living in Sabbath.

The walk back to the villa from town was uneventful. Uneventful in a good way. They were simply enjoying each other's company without having to say a word.

"Cooper," Asa broke the silence as they ducked through the narrow gate opening at the back of the villa property, "I have truly enjoyed our time together. You are now ready for whatever your journey has for you. You are prepared for your next assignment."

"Thank you, Asa. That is very special for me to know that you believe in me. You are an excellent mentor and counselor. You are my coach. I can truthfully say that our time together has changed my life."

"I will be leaving soon. It is possible that we will not enjoy our coffee together in the near future. I have other assignments to attend to. But I sincerely hope our paths cross again," Asa said softly as he reached out to hug Cooper.

Cooper felt a small amount of sadness as they embraced, but he felt a warmth and comfort that was difficult to describe.

"Thank you. I will never forget you," Cooper said as they stepped away from each other.

"I will be with you always, Cooper. Please remember that even though you may not be with me physically, we are always connected spiritually," Asa turned and went into his cottage leaving Cooper staring at the door. He took a deep breath and turned to walk up the hill to the villa.

Cooper Travis had no idea what he should do next. He spent the day after Christmas sleeping and relaxing in the villa. As he ate breakfast the next morning, Cooper stared down toward Asa's cottage hoping to see a stream of smoke coming up out of the pipe. In a cam and steady voice he read from the card that was laying on the table in front of him.

Act of Peace

Peace exists when Love & Faith dominate one's soul. That allows an individual to abide in a place of rest. Rest occurs when there is no conflict between the spirit, the soul, and the body. Peace is not a place or an event. Nor is it taken or earned. It is received. It is a state of being. Peace is Rest. Rest is Sabbath. Sabbath is Shalom. Shalom is Peace.

I am at peace.

I am anxious for nothing.

I am content with my past and I do not stress about my future.

I enjoy today and live in the moment.

I live a life of Sabbath. Sabbath is not a day or time; it is how I operate. It is the state of allowing my spirit to be in control and forcing my soul and body to obey.

I believe in God and I allow Love to flow through me. Therefore, I am at Rest.

My life is a life of Sabbath. I live a life of Shalom.

I am at Peace.

Everything was still except for a small breeze blowing up from the valley below where the river flowed. Cooper felt the cool air that the breeze was bringing with it.

It would be nice to enjoy Asa's company...and his coffee right now.

For the next few hours, he just sat on the veranda alone with his thoughts. But his thoughts were simple and basic. He was relaxed, feeling at peace, and anxious for nothing.

"Would it be possible for me to just stay here?" Cooper whispered out loud.

No sooner had those words exited his mouth when loud knocking reverberated throughout the entire villa. Cooper jumped to his feet with the realization that the sound of knocking was no longer familiar to him.

He walked briskly through the main living area to the front door. He swung the door open wide and gasped at the sight of TR and Angel standing there. The look of shock and relief on their faces surely mirrored his.

"Oh, thank God, it's you!" TR blurted out.

28

When his day had started a few hours earlier, Cooper never dreamed he would be standing in the foyer of the villa talking with Angel and TR. But here they were.

"Angel. TR. You have no idea how good it is to see you. How did you find me?"

TR explained how he and Angel had stayed in contact over the last few months, "When you failed to answer your phone or messages, I contacted the property manager in South Padre, and he discovered your stuff and the smashed phone. We had no clue where you were. I attempted to get local law enforcement involved, but they refused to spend resources on what was considered a federal fugitive case and not a missing person case."

Cooper noticed Angel staring at him while TR was doing all the talking. She even gave him a slight smile. *Hope. Hope is a powerful force.*

"In early October, we both got a mysterious note that said you were okay and safe and that we would get more details later. It was really odd," TR continued explaining their adventure. "Then on Christmas Eve we both received another note requesting that we go to Costa Rica to pick you up on December 27. It was a miracle that we were able to get last minute flights during the holidays, but here we are. Just like picking up a teenager after summer camp," TR chuckled to help cut the tension in the air.

"Your sentencing is next week in Houston," Angel said softly, "Samuel is hopeful there will be no negative repercussions if you are there as ordered."

"Then we will be in Houston next week. I am prepared for whatever the courts rule."

"We were hopeful that would be your response. We arranged transportation to pick us up first thing in the morning, and we have flights leaving from Alajuela early afternoon," TR explained the itinerary to Cooper.

"We may have an issue, however. I...uh...traveled down here without any papers, passport, or identification," Cooper held up his hand to stop any questions. "Do not ask me how that happened. Miracles piled up one after another. I honestly thought my journey would be cut short every step of the way. It was as if someone was orchestrating every move. So, basically, I do not have any identification that may allow me to get back into the US."

"Well, that issue may be solved. We had the property manager send your stuff to me. I have your passport and ID in my bag," TR said.

"Excellent, then all is well," Cooper began walking toward the doors that led to the veranda. He motioned for the others to follow, "That gives us this afternoon and evening to enjoy this beautiful villa. I am not sure I can be a good host, but the views are nice from the veranda. Let's go sit, relax, and chat."

When he stepped through the doorway, he spotted three trays on the table. *I wasn't even inside for ten minutes.*

"Were you expecting us?" Angel asked.

"I was expecting nothing. But it does appear that the fairy that has been serving me knew we would be having guests. Let's have lunch, shall we?"

While they ate, TR and Cooper did most of the talking. Angel sat quietly, and Cooper assumed she was processing all that was going on. Every time he caught her staring at him, she looked down after a few seconds.

The conversation drifted from what TR's family was doing to the national and world news Cooper had missed while being secluded. Then he tried to explain some of the events of the last few months, but he struggled to put them into words.

"Is it possible for us to see this Asa?" TR asked.

Cooper gazed down the hill toward the cottage, "Smoke coming from the chimney of his cottage has always been my cue to visit. And as you can see, there is nothing there. But we can go down to the cottage just to peek inside," Cooper sensed that TR and Angel were questioning some of his story. Perhaps if they could meet Asa or see inside the cottage, his story would have more credibility.

After lunch, Cooper gave TR and Angel a brief tour of the villa grounds, and they finished at the door of Asa's cottage. Before knocking, Cooper paused and told them how his time in this cottage was some of the most powerful of his life. The coaching he received from Asa. The warm fireside chats. And, of course, the best coffee he had ever had in his life.

"It would be nice to see inside this mecca of wisdom," TR said. Angel continued looking at Cooper, but she nodded in agreement with TR.

"Well, let's knock first just to see if he is around," Cooper hesitated as the words came out of his mouth. He tapped softly on the door. When he heard no response, he knocked a little louder. And then he reached down to see if the doorknob would turn. He slowly turned the knob and leaned into the door. At first the door did not move, so he leaned a little harder before stumbling into the cottage.

Cooper swiped at the cobwebs that immediately stuck to his face. Dust and cobwebs covered the entire interior of the main room. He slowly walked to the center of the cottage while wiping away the webs from his face and shoulders. He turned to look at Angel and TR standing outside peeking through the doorway at a room that showed no signs of human activity in years.

"I was just here two days ago. There was a fire in the fireplace. We sat in these rocking chairs. We drank coffee that was made on that counter. And those shelves were full of books," Cooper pointed and spoke as if he were an attorney presenting evidence to defend himself.

"Well, I am no expert," TR glanced over at Angel, but her eyes were fixed on Cooper, "But those shelves are empty now, and there has not been a fire in that fireplace for years. It looks like your friend Asa may have moved out. And from the looks of it, he moved out twenty years ago."

Cooper heard the snarkiness in TR's voice and attempted to make sense of the situation without really knowing what to say, "I cannot explain any of this. In fact, there are many things that I can't explain from the last four months of my life. I do not think it was a dream, and I am somewhat confident that I am not crazy," He paused and took a deep breath. *Was I dreaming? Everything made sense to me a few hours ago. Now I am beginning to question everything.* "I know this seems odd. But I spent mornings and evenings in this cottage. As strange as it sounds, everything has changed for me. I have learned about Love, Faith, and Peace. You have to believe me. Do you?" Cooper knew he was grasping for some validation.

TR's expression did not give Cooper any comfort. In fact, he looked a little irritated by the entire situation.

Angel smiled at Cooper and simply said, "I believe you."

As she had done many times, she provided exactly what Cooper needed at exactly the right time. And despite his doubts, her smile and simple statement gave him a short burst of energy.

"Are you two up for a walk to town? The path through the forest is nice and relaxing, and we can visit some friends of mine there. Maybe they can clear up the cobwebs," Cooper laughed nervously and pulled the cottage door closed behind him.

Angel nodded yes.

"If it is okay with you," TR said, "I would like to try out that sofa in the main house and catch a nap."

He just wants to avoid more weirdness from his old friend. Or maybe he's giving me some alone time with Angel. The excitement and nervousness inside him built as he thought about the long walk to town and back with Angel. She had been so quiet. *How can I tell her all that I need to say?*

But first he had to make sure everything was okay with TR, "Are you okay? You seem a little irritated."

"I'm sorry, Coop. I probably am a little irritated, tired, and grouchy. Jumping on a plane to Central America right after Christmas may have shaken my system. Let me get a nap, and I'll be in a better mood," TR started walking back up the hill.

"Are you sure you are up for a long walk?" Cooper asked Angel, "It will be about an hour each way."

"Sure," she said as she briefly touched his arm.

Cooper watched TR walking up toward the main house. He yelled, "Enjoy your nap."

"Enjoy your walk," TR yelled back without turning around.

29

"It sure is nice to see you," Angel said.

"I have no words to describe how much I have missed you," Cooper stood with his back to the cottage door he had just closed. He looked deep into her eyes before turning to his left and walking to the gate at the back of the property. He was just about to warn Angel about the need to stoop down and walk through the small opening when he noticed something different.

The bigger gate doors were cracked open. He reached for the gate handle and gave a soft push. The large door opened wide to show the path that cut through the woods. He turned back to Angel and smiled. He made the decision to not mention the odd circumstances about the small door being the only entry and exit for the last few months.

Cooper was calm, but his mind raced with so many things he felt he needed to say. Yet, something inside him caused him to pause and just walk.

He did tell Angel about his first time walking down the path. He pointed out the bridge as they passed. He also told her that the path on the other side of the bridge led to the coffee fields.

Perhaps I should go check to see if they are still there. Maybe, when we get to town, Juan and Pooh's house will be abandoned also. If that's the case, I might be able to plead insanity at my sentencing next week.

While these thoughts danced around in his mind, he wondered what Angel was thinking. Their conversation turned back to small talk about the weather in Aspen and Texas.

When they reached the town square, Cooper was relieved to see the church was still there and everything appeared to be the same as it had been forty-eight hours ago. They continued past the town square to Juan's house.

"Señor Travis, it is good to see you again," Juan said as the door swung open.

Cooper wondered if his relief was visible as Juan gave him a bear hug.

"Hello, Juan. I apologize for bothering you today. But I was wondering if I could ask you a few questions," Cooper said.

"Si. Come in," Juan replied and stepped back inside.

Cooper stepped aside to allow Angel to enter first.

"And who is this beautiful lady, Señor Travis?"

"I apologize. This is..." Cooper hesitated briefly, "This is Angel."

"Oh, this is your wife? You are blessed man to have beautiful woman," Juan said loud enough to be heard in the town square.

Angel blushed slightly and lowered her head.

Juan's wife walked out of the kitchen after hearing Juan's proclamation, and Pooh's door flew open a few seconds later. Cooper expected her to run and jump into his arms like she had done dozens of times, but instead she came to a halt beside her father when she spotted Angel.

"Angel, this is my wife Elizabeth and daughter Rosa Angelica. Our two sons are out enjoying the weather."

"Most of us call her Pooh," Cooper said as he looked to Angel and then back down to Pooh.

"My wife does not speak English. She has difficulty understanding conversation," Juan said.

Angel nodded, looked over at Elizabeth, and began speaking Spanish at a speed that was far beyond Cooper's skill level. Juan joined in, the conversation in Spanish flew around the room between the three of them.

Pooh stood by her father's side as she looked back and forth between Angel and Cooper. He reached out his hand and Pooh slowly walked over to take his hand. Together they walked over to stand near the sofa on the far wall. When he turned around, Cooper saw Angel hugging Elizabeth and Juan.

"They seem to be getting along well," Cooper said to Pooh.

"Yes, they are. She is very pretty," Pooh replied.

"Yes, she is. Just like you," Cooper smiled at Pooh, and she seemed to relax and go back to her spunky self.

"Is this a short visit? Or will you be staying for supper?"

Before he could answer, the others ceased talking and walked over toward them.

"Señor Travis, what can I answer? Please sit, and let's speak," Juan motioned toward the sofa and chairs.

"We would love to sit and visit for a short time. But we walked here, and we will need to walk back before it gets very late. Thank you for being so hospitable," Cooper said.

"I can drive you to villa and you stay and eat," Juan said as he looked over at Elizabeth.

"Thank you again. But it would be best if we walked back," Cooper said as he glanced at Angel.

Juan nodded as if to say he understood.

"I wanted to ask you some questions about our friend Asa," Cooper stated.

"Si, I will answer if I can."

"I was curious how long you have known Asa? And do you know much of his story and background?" Cooper asked.

"I not know much more than you. We saw him first during harvest last year. He was helpful and asked could he work again. He was great worker. Always showed up on time and no complain. We said yes, please come work next year. He stopped to visit during summer and said he stay in cottage on friend's property and he help with new harvest. He also say he had guest from States that stay on property. That be you. How did you meet?" Juan asked.

"I only met him once I arrived here. A few weeks before the harvest started," Cooper replied as he looked over to Angel again.

"Well, he act like he knew you. He ask if we knew a person to make food and clean for you. Elizabeth's cousin Maria volunteer after conversation with Asa. She says he sweet man so she help in any way that she can. She says she help with his mission. Whatever that means. You meet Maria?" Juan paused to ask a question.

"I did meet her, yes, but only once. She does a great job of staying hidden. But please let her know that I appreciate all that she did to serve me during my visit. We had a language barrier that made it difficult to communicate," Cooper said.

"Si, we let her know."

"I checked Asa's cottage today," Cooper hesitated and looked over at Angel again, "It appears as if he has already left."

"Si," Juan replied. "He stop yesterday as he leave. He say his assignment here finished, but he see us again in future. He say we not together physically, but we always connected spiritually. And then he leave."

"I am not sure what to say. I want to ask more questions, but I am not sure what to even ask," Cooper shrugged his shoulders as he spoke. *How do I process what Juan just said? Will this help prove that I'm not crazy in Angel's eyes?*

Juan suddenly jumped up, exclaimed something in Spanish, and walked over to a cabinet next to the front door. Cooper looked at Pooh for help in interpreting what Juan had just said.

"He said he almost forgot that Asa left something for you," She raised her eyebrows and grinned.

Perhaps he wrote a goodbye letter! This could explain all the strange circumstances from the last few months so Angel will believe me!

Juan started speaking in Spanish again, and Pooh continued translating, "In all the excitement of our last day of harvest, I forgot to pay both of you. This is your payment. When I tried to pay Asa, he insisted I give you his payment. It is not much. But it is the going rate for harvest work."

Juan handed two envelopes to Cooper.

Cooper held the envelopes stuffed with Costa Rican colones, "As much as I appreciate the payment because I may need some money in the near future," Cooper said as he looked over at Angel again, "I would prefer you give all of this to Maria."

Angel smiled and nodded in agreement.

"Are you sure, Señor Travis?" Juan asked.

"Yes, my stay in this area will never be forgotten. And her service to me was a big part of that," Cooper replied.

Juan turned to Elizabeth and told her what had just transpired. Elizabeth threw her hands in the air, brought them to her cheeks, blurted out something in Spanish, and ran to Cooper with her arms wide open. Cooper quickly stood to embrace her in a big hug. She was only slightly taller than Maria so her face was buried in Cooper's chest just above his belly. She stayed buried there as Pooh translated her Spanish.

"She says that your gift will be such a blessing to her cousin. She is a widow and you have given her enough money to live for a year."

Cooper smiled from ear to ear as Elizabeth backed away. Words could not express what was in his heart. However, the pause in the conversation and activity signaled that their visit was coming to an end. He looked down at Pooh and said, "I will be leaving tomorrow. I guess we need to say goodbye."

"Thank you for helping my papa with the harvest..." Pooh looked up at him with tears forming in her brown eyes, "and thank you for being my friend."

"I will miss you," Cooper said with a sudden catch in his voice.

"Don't worry, we will see each other again. You and Papa are going to have a business together selling coffee. Now give me a hug."

Cooper gave her a perplexed look before he knelt down on his knees and embraced her. Her arms clenched around his neck in a strong hug. Cooper knew neither of them wanted to let go. Through Pooh's dark hair that covered most of his face, Cooper could see tears streaming down Angel's cheeks.

The walk back to the villa was quiet. Cooper had no idea what to say next, and he was confident Angel did not know either.

As they turned off the dirt road onto the trail that led up to the villa, Angel reached out to gently hold Cooper's hand. At that moment, words flooded Cooper's mind. There was so much he wanted to say. So much that he needed to tell her. He felt so much shame for the way he had acted in the past, but he did not know how to share those thoughts.

When they approached the bridge, Cooper pulled on Angel's hand and guided her to the middle of the bridge.

"I have enjoyed this spot. It is so peaceful. The warmth from the late afternoon sun meeting the coolness from the water. This is the place where I finally admitted my belief in God and surrendered to Him," Cooper pulled Angel into his arms. "There is so much I need to tell you. So much I need to apologize for. You have been so patient with me. And I have abused your love and patience. Can you ever forgive me?"

"Shhh," Angel interrupted as she leaned in and put her index finger to his lips. "What I can feel from your heart speaks louder than any words that can come from your mouth," she whispered as she held his face with both hands and kissed him. She stood back and looked him in the eyes, "I have not been able to take my eyes off you since I arrived. You have changed physically, but I can tell that your soul has also been transformed and it has caused my love for you to grow beyond anything that I have ever known. I am so proud of the man that you have become."

And she kissed him again.

Cooper felt as if his entire body was melting and running into the cool water flowing beneath his feet.

30

"I feel like I am at a country club," TR said as he looked around the manicured grounds and park-like setting.

"I am not sure a federal prison would be considered a country club," Cooper chuckled, "but some do call this place Club Fed. It's ranked in the top ten cushiest prisons in the federal system."

A slight breeze blew through Cooper's short hair. The day was warmer than normal for late February in Pensacola, and the sun warmed both TR and Cooper while they sat at a picnic table on the grounds of the federal prison.

"How are Hannah and the girls?" Cooper asked.

"They are doing great, and they want you to know they are thinking about you and praying for you. Becca says you can come stay in her bedroom anytime you want. And she finally has her front teeth, so we can understand her better."

"That is great. Tell her I would love to come visit her. Her Dora the Explorer bed would be much better than my current one," Cooper paused as he thought back to how much his life had changed in six short months since he first visited TR's house.

The two men sat in silence for a few seconds. They both took deep breaths and sighed in unison.

"So, how are you really doing?" TR asked.

"Well, this is still a prison, so to say it is the most pleasant experience in the world would be a lie. But all things considered, I am thriving."

"Thriving? In prison?"

"Yes, that is a word and principle I learned while in Costa Rica," Cooper hesitated before saying more. He knew TR was still unsure about Asa, and he did not want to scare away his first visitor while in prison. "I am reading more than I ever have in my life. Expanding my knowledge and thought process beyond just the business world and making money. I signed up for a Spanish class, and I get my work assignment soon."

"Work assignment?"

"Yes, we actually work and make money. I think it is fifteen cents per hour, and I am hopeful I can work inside, but since I have experience harvesting coffee and working on a plantation, I may get some landscaping duty. I actually enjoyed working outside so much when I was in Costa Rica that I think I would enjoy just working out in the sun and heat."

"You know, I am still confused by all that happened with your trial and sentencing. How long are you going to be here?" TR asked.

"I am not sure I can really explain it either. Samuel called it a miracle. I have had so many miracles recently I just believe that someone is watching over me and taking care of me. But when we originally began the plea bargain process a year ago, we were hopeful I would serve thirty-six months or less. That is a reasonable sentence for mail fraud—"

"Sorry for interrupting, but I really don't understand the mail fraud charge. What exactly is that? You didn't get in trouble for mailing something, did you?"

"Not exactly. And I was confused, too. It seems that mail fraud is a catch all for business crimes that may be perceived as deceptive or fraudulent. Since mail and email cross state lines, it becomes a federal crime that is easy to prove. We were promoting our products aggressively online and doing follow-up campaigns using mail. And when you are making claims that can't be backed up or cause people harm, it is easy to say you are committing fraud."

"Sounds harsh."

"I guess. Going back to your question of how long I'm in for, one of the most interesting things about being in prison is the type of people in here. Most are white collar criminals, but a few are drug dealers or worse. But no matter their crime, every prisoner falls into one of two categories. The innocent ones and the guilty ones. At least some think they are innocent. And you know which group they are in within just a few minutes of meeting them."

"Which group are you in?" TR smiled as he asked.

"Guilty. Guilty with a capital G. And I have no one to blame but myself. Sure, there were others in the company that pushed rules and regulations and broke laws, but as the CEO, it all comes back to me."

"You still haven't said how long your sentence is."

"True. Hear me out," Cooper smiled, "For the first year, I was in denial and pretty obnoxious about everything. But when you guys brought me back from Costa Rica for the final sentencing, I had a level of humility that I had never experienced or shown before. For some reason, I think that had an impact on the judge. So, for whatever reason, I wasn't even sentenced to the full thirty-six months in prison. I have to serve eight months followed by two years of supervised release."

"Sounds like you are excited about that?"

"Definitely. I am grateful for that and so many other things. The company entered bankruptcy, and everyone felt some restitution should be paid to those that were deceived or harmed. Obviously, we had no way of paying all those claims, and the judge could have made me personally liable. Fortunately, the company still had some really cool technology that had value, and another company swooped in at the last minute. They agreed to purchase our assets. And as part of their price, they settled all our claims."

"Wow. That is definitely a blessing!"

"Don't get me wrong, Angel and I have very little money. But at least I get to keep the fifteen cents per hour I make here in prison so I can live a good life. When I am released, we will be at zero. Or maybe a few dollars above zero. But that is better than spending the rest of our lives paying restitution. That is a miracle, and I am excited."

"Well then, I am excited for you also. As excited as I can be with my old friend in prison."

"I understand. We still have a tough road ahead. But I messed up and there is a price to pay. My prayer is that those I have hurt can eventually forgive me."

TR stared at Cooper and then grinned for a few seconds before speaking, "You have changed. The old Cooper Travis would never ask for forgiveness or even admit he was wrong about anything. Probably because you could do no wrong."

Cooper let TR's words float around him in the Florida breeze. He really did feel like a different person.

"Thankfully, Angel seems to have forgiven me. She is such a compassionate woman that has always stood by me. It amazes me at times how I have never even sensed a hint of regret or remorse from her. She really understands the *Act of Love* and has the ability to give it without any expectation of return. We still have much to work through after the way I treated her, but all I can do is show her as much love as possible."

"Is she still in Texas?" TR asked.

"She is for now. She is selling most of what we own. The personal debts piled up over the last year, and we decided to liquidate as much as we can and prepare to start over. We think we will have enough after everything is sold for her to get a small apartment near here so that we can be closer to each other. I miss her. We have also decided...or I guess I can say that I have finally embraced the idea of us having children and starting a family. She has wanted that for so long, and I ignored her desires because of my selfishness. Not sure how that will work while I am incarcerated, but we have at least agreed to try," Cooper chuckled as he attempted to make a joke.

"Children are great. I think they show us how God sees us."

"Six months ago, I would have disagreed or just said children really should not be brought into this world. But then I met your girls, and on my journey south, it seemed as if children were being placed in my path just so my heart could be softened. A young girl helped me cross into Mexico, and Pooh absolutely stole my heart. That was another miracle that I would have never imagined," Cooper paused as he contemplated changing the conversation "Can I ask you a question about your dad?"

"Coach? Sure?" TR looked at him with a curious expression on his face.

"Do you know anything about the person he met when he was in South Padre? When you said everything changed for him?"

"Funny you bring that up. I've thought about your mysterious friend Asa quite a bit over the past few weeks. Honestly, I was really tired and grumpy that day, and I thought you were possibly going crazy. But when we were flying back to Texas, I started thinking how similar Asa sounded to what Coach described. At the time, you seemed as if you had been transformed by your relationship with Asa. I don't think I have any answers, but your stories do sound similar. Do you think the situations are related?"

"Well, I don't know. I can't deny that I had a strong urge to go to your place in South Padre."

"That was a little weird for Hannah and me. We were talking on the back porch, and then suddenly you wanted to go to our beach house."

"It is hard to describe what I felt. But when you are spiraling down and something gives you a glimmer of hope, you seize it as quickly as you can. I had no hope. When you insisted I come to Coach's funeral, it was the last thing I wanted to do. But it was exactly what I needed. I think that was the jolt that set me on the path I am on now. I know I am in prison and things do not look great on the outside, but I am at peace on the inside."

"And that's what matters, my friend."

"I think it is important that I say this. I appreciate you insisting that I come to the funeral and stay with you and your family. That was a significant day in my journey," Cooper's voice choked. "You may have saved my life."

"Time to wrap it up, guys," a stern voice interrupted their conversation, "You have one minute."

"Coop, all I wanted at the time was to reconnect with my old friend. I thought we might be able to have some kind of relationship. I knew you were going through some tough times, but I had no idea they were as bad as they actually were," TR's eyes started to water as he finished his sentence.

"Well, we have reconnected. You may be the only person that wants to be associated with me," Cooper said as they both stood up from the table.

They started walking along the path toward the main building. After a few steps, Cooper paused and looked at the guard hoping to gain a few extra seconds. When the guard nodded, Cooper stood up straight and stepped closer to TR.

"TR, please forgive me. I abandoned our friendship in pursuit of money and business success, and I regret doing that to you. We were friends, and I was just selfish. I never should have allowed my ambitions to come between us," there was a small catch in his voice, "Thank you for this visit and please consider forgiving me."

TR looked over at the guard and then reached out to wrap his arms around Cooper. The two men stood in a tight embrace as tears started streaming down their faces.

"Coop, my friend, I do forgive you. Hannah and the girls forgive you. I hope that others forgive you also."

The guard's tap on Cooper's shoulder signaled the end to their visit.

31

"Pura vida, Juan. I'm learning Spanish now, but I don't think I know enough to speak it in conversation with you yet," Cooper spoke loudly on the video call.

"No problem, Señor Travis," Juan replied, "I am ok to speak with you in any language. Pooh has helped improve my English. How have you been since we saw you four months ago?"

"As well as expected considering I moved to prison on the twentieth of January. I know Angel has kept in contact with you about my situation, but I wanted to speak to you myself and try to explain."

"You have nothing to explain to me. We all make mistake, and we all need forgiveness. You helped me during harvest, and for that I am always grateful."

"I cannot begin to tell you how much that means to me. Thank you for your unconditional love. That is rarer than I ever knew."

"My pleasure. Now, can I ask you favor? When I was emailing with your wife, I told her that if you able to speak I would be honored. I was pleased when she sent a message saying you would have time soon where you would be free for a few hours."

"Yes, I was also pleased you wanted to speak. Furlough days from prison are rare. But Angel recently moved into an apartment nearby, so I was able to get a few hours away from the prison," Cooper reached across the small kitchen table to hold Angel's hand, "What is the favor you ask of me?"

"I know you are a great businessman—"

"Remember I am in prison because of some mistakes I made in business."

"Si, yes, Señor Travis. I know that but I have seen your heart. And how you treat my children."

Cooper's mind wandered as he thought of Pooh. He tried to focus again on what Juan was saying.

Juan continued, "I really think you can help us with business. You have been here. You know how hard people work. You know how good our beans are. You worked in our fields. You know American business. Can you help?"

Cooper had known this day was coming before he even left Costa Rica. He had a vision of how they could continue to give away most of the coffee and just take ten percent of the crops to sell and build the business. "Thank you for asking. I can help. However, I can only give you free advice at this time. We are not permitted to participate in a business while in prison. I will consult with you, and we can communicate via email until I am released. After prison, I will be on supervised release, and I will find out if I can participate in the business legally."

"That is perfect, Señor Travis. Thank you! Thank you!" Juan exclaimed.

"Please call me Cooper if we are going to help each other. I will send you a message in the next few days with some questions, and we will begin our journey," Cooper smiled and realized he was filled with joy by this new opportunity.

"One more thing, Señor...I mean Cooper."

"Yes?"

"I have someone here that has been begging to say hello," Juan said. Pooh's face popped up on the video screen after she climbed on Juan's lap.

"Well, hello there!" Cooper couldn't help but grin when he saw his young friend's beautiful face in front of him.

"Hello," Pooh softly replied with a half smile.

"I have missed you and that beautiful Costa Rican British accent you have. How are you feeling?" Cooper realized he was gushing, but he didn't care.

"I feel fine," she replied.

"Her blood counts are perfect. She is healed," Juan piped in.

"Are you doing well?" Pooh asked softly.

"I am doing much better now that I am talking to you."

"When are you going to come back and visit me?" she asked.

"Well, actually I have something important to tell you and a favor to ask."

Pooh nodded, but didn't say anything.

"The time I spent with you and your family while I was in Costa Rica was some of the best times of my life. There were some things that I should have shared with you that I want you to know now."

Pooh tilted her head to the side as she waited.

Cooper tried his best to explain the complicated situation to his eight-year-old friend.

After a short pause, Pooh asked, "Are you sorry for what you did?"

Cooper let out a deep breath and looked over at Angel. "Yes. I am so sorry for these mistakes. I hate it that I have hurt those around me and disappointed them. It hurts me to have to tell people that I love like you that I am in jail for breaking the law."

"I am not disappointed in you. You are one of my best friends. Best friends love each other all the time. Even if they make mistakes," Pooh said matter of factly.

Cooper's eyes watered, and he let out a chuckle at the same time. "That is one of the best things that anyone has ever said to me. Thank you. Can I ask you a question?"

Pooh nodded in agreement again.

"I think it is important when people hurt others or make mistakes that they ask for forgiveness. Do you think you can forgive me?" Cooper pleaded.

Pooh smiled and her hesitation seemed to vanish. The personality he saw while harvesting coffee cherries appeared on his screen.

"Of course, you silly ole bear. I forgive you, and you will be my best friend for a long time. Maybe until we are a hundred years old or more," she said with the sassiness Cooper had grown to expect from her, "Are they being nice to you where you are staying?"

"They are being as nice as they should be. They feed us food that is not really good, but at least we have food. I sleep in a room with three other men. They make us wake up early, and we all have jobs. I trim hedges and rake at the Air Force base near us. I do have a little desk I can keep my books on. That is where I write. And guess what? I am learning Spanish in one of our classes. I am in school like you."

Pooh giggled, "That is funny that you are in school like me. Can you speak some Spanish to me?"

"Mi amiga Pooh es muy bonita y muy inteligente," Cooper spoke in a slow methodical tone, "I still have more to learn before I can really have a conversation."

"Gracias. Now, when are they going to let you out of that jail so you can come visit me? I can help you with your Spanish lessons."

"Well, I would love to come today, but I will be here for a few more months and then it may be difficult to travel for a few years. They let me leave for a few hours today to visit Angel in our apartment. She just moved here to Florida."

"Okay, well, I expect to see you here as soon as they say you can visit."

"Well, I am not sure if I should say something about this, but your father and I may be doing some work together and he may have to come to America. When he comes, you need to come with him."

Pooh's mouth opened wide, and she looked up at Juan.

Juan nodded and said, "Si, we may need to go."

"That would be excellent! You will have to show me everything I need to see in your country."

"Our country is pretty big, but we will do our best," Cooper glanced again at Angel. She was smiling, but she reached down to her watch and tapped it with her finger.

"I could talk to you all day, but I do have to go back soon. Can we talk again?" Cooper asked.

Both Pooh and Juan nodded in unison.

"Thank you both for being my friend. It means so much to me to have friends like you. I love you both so much and cannot wait to speak to you again."

"We love you, too," Pooh made a heart shape with her fingers, "Be nice to the other men in your prison room."

"I will," Cooper waved at the camera as the screen went dark.

Cooper sat staring at the blank screen for a few seconds before looking at Angel. He slid his other hand across the table, and Angel laid her hand on top of his.

"I love seeing how you and Pooh interact and talk to each other. It warms my heart seeing how soft and gentle you are with her."

"I do love her. I never thought I would have such a strong desire to be around children until my journey began last summer. I really do want us to begin our family soon. Do you think we can do that now? While I am in prison and you are here?" Cooper asked.

Angel's smile gave her answer without a word being spoken. They sat in silence for a few seconds before Angel spoke, "I have to ask you to forgive me now."

Cooper furrowed his brow. "For what, my Angel?"

"I have been keeping a secret from you for the last few months," Angel flashed the smile that always made him weak in the knees, "You are going to be a father, Cooper Travis."

Cooper's mouth fell open. He knew the shock and joy was registering on his face. He jumped up and pulled Angel into a hug. They both wiped tears from their eyes as they leaned back to look at each other.

"I know you have been saying you were ready to start our family since your return from Costa Rica. But I was not sure if you really meant it. I think your reaction tells me you are excited?" Angel said through her tears.

"Yes! Yes! A thousand times yes! This is the best news ever. Thank you, Lord," Cooper looked up at the ceiling through his tears. "How? How did this happen? When did this happen?"

"Well, Cooper, you are almost forty years old. I would hope I do not have to explain to you how this happened," Angel grinned and winked. "As to the when, the doctor thinks we may have conceived during the last few days of December. I believe it was that night in the villa before we brought you back to the US."

Cooper was at a loss for words. *I'm going to be a father!*

Angel continued, "I have known since mid-February not long after you went to prison. I did not want to tell you over the phone or email, so I was really hoping you would get this furlough day so I could tell you in person."

"Are you okay? Is everything good? Will it be okay for you to stay here in this small apartment while you are pregnant?" A thousand questions flooded his mind.

"I am fine, and this apartment will be the perfect place for us to start our family. If the doctor's math is correct, Baby Travis will arrive about the time you are released."

"That would be great. I do not want to miss this," Cooper said as he stepped back and gently placed a hand on Angel's stomach.

"I have another surprise for you," Angel grinned as she looked up from his hand on her stomach and into his eyes.

"I'm not sure I can handle another surprise today. This day is already the best day of my life. What else could make it better?" he gushed.

"I have an appointment at the doctor's office today before you go back. They are planning to do an ultrasound. If all goes well, we may get to see our baby together for the first time."

32

Cooper's mind raced, not about business or making money or his massive list of things he should be doing as it would have in the past.

I'm going to be a father.

Had he known this eight months ago, he would have been terrified. Possibly even annoyed because it was not something he was controlling. Today, he was bubbling over with joy as he sat in the waiting room with Angel. Uncontrollable, childlike, giddy joy.

"Are you feeling good? Have you been eating anything special? Can you tell if something is growing in there?" Cooper had been peppering Angel with questions since she shared the news.

Angel sighed a deep breath as she held his hand, "I love all these questions. All this attention. It is new for me to have all your energy focused on me."

She stopped, took another deep breath while squeezing his hand even harder and stared at him for a brief moment before continuing.

"But don't get me wrong, I love it and appreciate it. And I am fine. I feel good. I am watching what I eat, and I am confident Baby Travis is doing well also. Relax and let's enjoy this together."

"Everything is looking good with the mother. The technician will use this machine to see if we can see the baby. It is a little late for your first ultrasound, isn't it?" Dr. James asked Angel.

"We have had some life transitions that we are working through," Angel replied as she glanced over at Cooper.

"I am serving time in the prison here, and she was selling our home in Texas and moving to an apartment here in Pensacola," Cooper added a few more details to Angel's explanation.

Dr. James paused, but his expression did not change. "Did you bust out to make this appointment today?" Dr. James winked at Angel.

"Well, I would have, but somehow I was able to get a furlough day only ninety days into my sentence. I hope to be released before this baby comes."

"I am glad things worked out for you to be here. We don't see as many fathers as we should. The mother is doing great," he smiled at Angel. "But other than being in prison, how is the father doing?"

"When one makes a mistake, there are consequences. But as tough as it is, this news today makes this the best day of my life. The only thing that would make it better is if you can guarantee our baby will arrive after the twentieth of September."

Dr. James shot a puzzled look at Cooper and then Angel.

"That is his release date," Angel replied.

"Do you happen to know when you conceived?"

"Most likely the night of December 27," Angel blushed as she replied.

Dr. James tapped on his tablet.

"It will be very close. If your date is accurate, the models say the third week of September. But we consider a few things when estimating a due date. Let's have Jenny do the ultrasound and get some measurements. That will give us a better estimate of how far along you are," He reached out to shake Cooper's hand, "Congratulations, again."

Cooper sat at eye level to Angel's abdomen, "I do see a little bump now. How did I not notice it before?"

Jenny spread a gooey substance on Angel's belly, "Let's see if this baby cooperates."

Cooper rested his chin on Angel's arm and stared at the screen on the other side of the table. His hand gripped Angel's.

Jenny placed a wand on Angel's abdomen and swoosh, swoosh, swoosh sounds filled the room, "That is your baby's heartbeat. It sounds good and strong."

Cooper squeezed Angel's hand even harder and reached up to touch her cheek softly with his other hand. They watched the screen as Jenny moved the wand around and explained what they were looking at. Through the fuzziness on the screen, an image began materializing. First a head and then the rest of the body.

"Do you want to know the sex?" Jenny asked.

Cooper looked at Angel who gave Cooper a small nod.

"Sure. Can you do that?" he asked.

"We will see. It is a little early to be absolutely certain unless I can get a clear view, but we can get lucky at times. From the size and measurements, I am estimating your delivery date will be late September."

Cooper and Angel quickly turned their heads and locked eyes on each other.

"Let's say September 20. The gender is a little more of a guess. But I can tell you that I do not see any boy parts. So maybe seventy-five percent sure it will be a girl. This is your child," Jenny held her hand still and pointed to the monitor.

Cooper stared at the image wiggling on the screen. He leaned his head toward Angel and kissed her forehead.

"Thank you," he said as he kissed her forehead again.

The sun set slowly over the emerald green water and white sugary sand of Florida's panhandle.

"The colors of the sunset will take your breath away," Angel said as she and Cooper leaned on the hood of the car at the end of the day, "It's become one of my favorite things about this area of Florida."

"I can see why. It's beautiful," Cooper replied.

"Could you ever live here?" Angel asked.

"You mean voluntarily live here? If the days are anything like this, it may be tough for me to leave."

"Things are so different now. It almost seems as if we should just start our lives over in a new place."

"I do agree things are different. I feel completely changed. I can't even believe who I have become in less than a year. I just want to be wherever you and our baby will be, my Angel, but this would be a great spot. If this wasn't a park, it would be great to have a piece of land here."

"I am not sure our budget can afford beachfront property. My little two-bedroom apartment is a stretch after all of the legal costs and other expenses."

"I am sorry about the money situation," Cooper wrapped his arm around his wife, "It may be tough for us to live off of my prison landscaping salary and the small amount of money left in the bank. I hate it that you may have to work."

"Stop it. No whining about our situation. You know I have always said I never loved you for money or material things," Angel's tone was strong. "We still have a little money from selling the house. I know we will be okay."

Cooper smiled as he rested his head against hers, "I love it that you know we will be okay. I'm not pleased with how everything happened, but I am excited about starting over."

"I do want you to know how proud I am to be married to you. I have always loved you since you convinced me I should," Angel chuckled, and Cooper couldn't help but laugh out loud with her. "Since Costa Rica you are a different man. I love who you have become, Cooper Travis. Someday you will need to share how you were transformed while we were apart."

"I am still on that journey. And a journey is the best way to describe it. I cannot explain everything that happened. Especially how I ended up in Costa Rica and met Asa. But I know that was critical to me becoming who I am now...Becoming the husband you need, the father that I need to be...And as you told me, the man God created me to be."

"You haven't said much about Asa since we left Costa Rica. It seemed odd that he was not there. Have you spoken with him?"

"No, I wish I could. It is hard to understand who or what he is. I think he was a real person, but he may have been a figment of my imagination. Or maybe an angel or maybe even God. He just wanted me to call him my coach. All I know is that he taught me three principles or *Acts*, as he called them, that have changed everything about who I am now and possibly even altered my future. Instead of being the selfish, obsessive, and stressed out man that I once was, I am now a man of love, faith, and peace," Cooper explained.

"Whatever it is, I love it."

"I do need to share something else with you before we head back to the prison," Cooper said with hesitation.

"What is it?"

"This is tough for me to admit even now, but last August, I...I considered...taking my own life," Cooper paused, unsure if he should continue. He felt Angel pull away from him and knew she was waiting for him to look at her. He slowly raised his eyes to meet hers. "I even went so far as to point a gun to my head and pull the trigger."

Angel's hands went quickly to her face, and she shook her head back and forth, "No, no, no. Please don't tell me that. August...that was when...oh, Cooper, was it my fault?"

"No, Angel, it was not your fault. It was all about me. I was selfish. The good thing is that something...or someone...kept the gun from working. I think my journey really started then," Cooper hesitated, "I also need to tell you something else."

Angel dropped one hand from her face and placed it on his arm as if to say she wanted to hear more but was fearful of what it might be.

"Don't worry, it's nothing else as crazy as a gun to my head. I was confused and thinking all kinds of crazy thoughts before I started my journey. This one thing was not really crazy, but it is significant. Asa taught me so much, but I think what he really did was guide me to make a decision. A powerful, life-altering decision. He forced me to admit that I do have faith. I do have belief. I have no doubt that God exists and that He created me for a purpose. Remember the bridge that we stood on after our walk into town?"

Angel dropped her hands and visibly relaxed. She simply nodded that she remembered.

"Well, I don't know if you remember, but I told you that was the place that I admitted my faith and I surrendered. I surrendered my arrogance and belief that I was the center of the universe. That day, I became a man of Love, Faith, and Peace. I once believed that I was a god. Now I believe in the one and only God," Cooper heard the strength in his own voice as he proclaimed his newfound beliefs to his wife.

"That is so beautiful. It may be the most beautiful thing you have ever told me."

"I have so much more to share with you about all that I learned, but I know our time is limited today. I do need to ask one more thing before we go," Cooper stepped in front of her and got down on one knee. He reached up to take her hands in his. "Will you forgive me? I have not been the husband you deserve and for that I ask you to forgive me. I know I will make mistakes, but I commit to being the husband to you that God would want me to be," he leaned in to put his face on her belly as the sun touched the horizon behind him, "And I commit to being the father that I was created to be. Will you forgive me, Angel Travis?"

Angel reached down to tilt his face up toward hers, "Yes. Yes. I forgive you. I love you, and I know you will be the best father ever. Now, let's get you back to the prison so you can finish up your time and get out before this baby is born."

33

Bright fluorescent light filled the room. Cooper had a slight smile on his face as he laid both hands on The Tablet that was sitting on the desk. His hand gently brushed the cover before he opened the journal and picked up his pen.

The Tablet – June 6

I am grateful.

I could not wish for anything more in my life at this time.

My Angel and I are enjoying a renewed passion for each other. Restoration has occurred in all areas of our relationship.

I am grateful.

My health is the best it has ever been. I have energy and I feel fit.

I am grateful.

Many things have changed in my financial and business life. My finances are much simpler now, but we have more than enough to live our lives. Plus the coffee business with Juan has the potential to be rewarding in many ways.

I am grateful.

The lessons that Asa taught me have changed my life. I will continue to meditate on them and let them sink into my soul.

Act of Love

Love is unearned, unconditional compassion and understanding for all people. It is not just a feeling or emotion. It is patient, kind, and honoring to others. Love is an action. It is something that one does. We are commanded to Love God and Love others as we Love ourselves.

I will show Love.

I will seek opportunities to honor those around me.

I have not earned the Love that is shown to me. Therefore, I will not expect others to earn Love from me.

I will not judge.

I will be quick to forgive.

I will be a person of compassion and understanding.

My thoughts, words, and actions will be evidence of the Love that flows through me at all times.

I will show Love.

Act of Faith

Faith is the unapologetic and unashamed belief that there is a God and that He is our creator. Faith is the confidence that God loves His creation and has a desire for us to thrive, flourish, and find our place in His world. Faith is hope in a better future and assurance that He has the power, wisdom, and the desire to help me follow His plan for my life.

I believe in God.

I am convinced; nothing can alter my conviction and belief in this truth.

I am not searching for answers. I know the answer. The answer is relationship with God.

I do not always understand His plan, but I know He has a plan and I have a role in it.

I place all my trust in Him.

I was created for a purpose. My assignment is to identify and accept that purpose.

I was not created to fail.

I was created to succeed.

I believe in God.

Act of Peace

Peace exists when Love & Faith dominate one's soul. That allows an individual to abide in a place of rest. Rest occurs when there is no conflict between the spirit, the soul, and the body. Peace is not a place or an event. Nor is it taken or earned. It is received. It is a state of being. Peace is Rest. Rest is Sabbath. Sabbath is Shalom. Shalom is Peace.

I am at peace.

I am anxious for nothing.

I am content with my past and I do not stress about my future.

I enjoy today and live in the moment.

I live a life of Sabbath. Sabbath is not a day or time; it is how I operate. It is the state of allowing my spirit to be in control and forcing my soul and body to obey.

I believe in God and I allow Love to flow through me. Therefore, I am at Rest.

My life is a life of Sabbath. I live a life of Shalom.

I am at Peace.

I am grateful.

Most of all, we are so blessed that we are expecting to be parents. I will have the joy of watching Baby Travis enter this world. Angel will be an amazing mother, and I will do everything in my power to be the loving and caring father that our child needs.

I am grateful.

I am at Peace.

Cooper looked up from the small desk and smiled. He had just finished writing on the last page of *The Tablet* that Angel had given him over a year ago. He closed it, placed his pen next to it, and leaned back in the small chair.

As soon as he let out a long breath, loud buzzer sounds signaled the time for the evening stand up count before lights out. For the past five days, he had been the only one in his cube that typically housed four inmates. He was enjoying the quiet in a prison system that was normally overcrowded.

After the count, he usually had ten to fifteen minutes before lights went out. This was the time that feelings of loneliness and isolation could overpower him, and he missed his Angel the most. Tonight, he sat back down at the desk by his cot, the only space he could call his own.

The Tablet sat in the center of the small metal desk. In it were ideas, thoughts, business plans. And of course, *The Acts* he had learned from Asa. One of those business plans was titled JC Coffee, and it included a unique structure to distribute coffee from Juan's coffee harvests.

On the corner of the desk was a stack of books. His Bible sat on top of the stack. Cooper had been attempting to read and study as much of it as he could. Asa had encouraged him to study the book that provided the foundation for the *Acts* that he had learned. His stack also included *The Greatest Salesman in The World,* the book that Asa had given him. He had read the book four times, and the message was exactly what Cooper needed to combine with Asa's lessons. The final book was the original *Winnie The Pooh*. He had read it a dozen times and found hidden gems and nuggets from the AA Milne classic every time he read it. And of course, it reminded him of Pooh.

Above his desk was a fuzzy image taped to the wall. Baby Travis's first photo. Cooper stared at the fuzzy picture. It was the most beautiful image he had ever seen in his life.

His heart was full. Even though he was serving a prison term, he could not remember a time in his life when he was more at peace. Rest. Shalom. Sabbath.

He pushed back from the desk and crossed the short distance to lay down on his small cot. As his head hit the pillow, he was startled by a hard object underneath it. He reached under the pillow and felt a small burlap bag. He pulled it out and almost lost his breath at the site and scent. He stood up and placed the bag on his desk before stepping over to the door. He looked around to see if anyone was near…if anyone was looking. He almost expected to see Asa standing in the corridor, but there was no one visible outside his cell. He turned around and sat down at the desk to check his surprise find.

He slowly untied the knot keeping the burlap bag closed. As the bag opened, the unmistakable scent of Asa's "special" coffee beans filled the air. Inside the large burlap bag was a small bag identical to the kind Asa used to grind and prepare his coffee. There was also a piece of metal slightly larger than a business card in the bag.

"I will have to get this approved," he said softly knowing that metal in prison was not always allowed.

He poked his nose down into the bag with the beans and took a long slow breath to enjoy the aroma. The smell was intoxicating. At times, he wondered if the smell of coffee beans was more enjoyable to him than the actual taste.

His mind raced back to the villa, the cottage, and the hours that he had spent sipping coffee and listening to Asa.

"Asa," His voice trailed off as his eyes got a little misty.

The metal piece glimmered in the light. He picked it up and read out loud the three words engraved on it, "Love. Faith. Peace."

Words that he had committed to continue studying and living for the rest of his life. A large smile came to his face as he reached down to put his hand on the journal. His fingers caressed the engraved title on the leather cover.

The Tablet

Be The Person God Created You To Be

He opened the journal to the third page. He laid the metal card down in the book under the four words he had written only nine months before.

The Tablet – September 13

God, I need you.

ACKNOWLEDGMENTS

I am sure that many people find great joy in writing. I want to be truthful and admit that writing this novel has stretched me beyond anything I could have imagined when the project started years ago.

On our podcast I will often ask authors what they learned about themselves during the writing process. The answers are fascinating and they have inspired me.

I cannot fully answer that question for myself here (check out our podcast or some of the bonus resources for the book) but I will say that this process has exposed weaknesses and strengths in me that I never knew existed. And for that I am thankful.

Even though writing involves hours and hours of just sitting and typing, the team that helps me coach, speak, podcast and now write has made all of this possible.

My daughter Dulce keeps everything organized and moving forward. I appreciate her diligence and attention to detail.

Her husband Hunter has recently helped with our web presence and other technical tasks and without him our SeekGoCreate video episodes would not be edited and up on YouTube.

Our son Joshua (JK) has edited 150 plus episodes of the SeekGoCreate podcast and he is credited with branding most of our projects.

There are so many people that have encouraged me to embrace education and the learning process. Both my parents were educators and I could fill up many pages with the teachers that have poured themselves into my future. At the risk of leaving some out, I do know that my high school English teachers Joanne Witherington, Margaret Fresola, and Marcia Stephenson would be excited and possibly surprised to see my name on the cover of this book..

As a coach myself, I recognized that I needed a coach to help with this project. Kara Starcher not only provided valuable editing but also gave feedback on plot points and character development. Some of the key aspects of the story came from her pointed and gentle feedback.

My wife Glori has been my partner and project manager for our lives since the mid '80's when we met. Her wisdom and skills have made every business, project and now this book possible. Thank you for your love and patience.

Some people may think it is odd when I say that portions of this book wrote itself. I believe that the story, the characters and much more are a product of divine inspiration. Some parts just flowed easily while others took more diligence and focus. I am so grateful that God gave me permission to write this story. He is my source and I am part of His Kingdom.

ABOUT THE AUTHOR

 Tim Winders is a Strategic Coach, Author, and host of SeekGoCreate, a podcast and YouTube interview show. He has worked in the areas of Leadership, Business, and Ministry for almost 40 years. Tim was the guy that looked like he had it all: the big house in a Country Club resort, two businesses valued at over a million dollars each, plus over $15 million in real estate. But, in 2008, the real estate markets crashed. After a slow and painful erosion of his companies, he and his wife were bankrupt and homeless living out of their Honda van by 2013.

Fast forward to today. Tim and his wife are still homeless, but they consider themselves essential nomads. They live, travel, and work in their 39-foot motor coach while enjoying the best locations North America has to offer. Through this journey, he is convinced that we must redefine success in order to live our best life. This topic is what he has explored with his guests on the SeekGoCreate podcast since 2019.

Tim is available for limited speaking engagements and leadership coaching. Connect with him at TimWinders.com.

RESOURCES

Break free from the addiction to more and embrace a life that is overflowing with love, faith and peace.

Add the Acts to your daily routine.

Get your screensaver downloads with the Act of Love, Act of Faith & Act of Peace along with other bonus resources using this QR code, or follow this link: https://timwinders.com/coachresources

———

Stay connected to Tim, his podcast, videos and social media channels at: https://seekgocreate.com

CPSIA information can be obtained
at www.ICGtesting.com
Printed in the USA
JSHW030936300422
25328JS00001B/18